THE SPIDER:
THE SPIDER STRIKES

MASTER OF MEN!

THE SPIDER STRIKES

By R.T.M. Scott

ALTUS PRESS • 2018

CHAPTER 1
THE MAN WHO
SOUGHT TO DIE

"I BELIEVE that the Spider is on this ship," remarked a pompous little man, waving a bundle of newspaper clippings.

In the smoke-room of the trans-Atlantic liner conversation lowered at mention of the mysterious New York criminal who sealed his deeds with the tiny design of a particularly hideous spider.

"And what makes you think that the Spider is on board?" somebody asked.

"These newspaper clippings," the little man exclaimed importantly. "A great criminal likes to keep a record of his crimes. I tell you that we might be murdered in our beds any night."

"Where did you find the clippings?" somebody else asked.

"Under a deck chair."

A young woman tittered as she raised her third before-dinner cocktail. "You shouldn't go poking under deck chairs," she remarked. "You might find things."

There were some smiles, but most faces were serious. The presence of the Spider was a most uncomfortable thought.

Richard Wentworth raised his well-built, lithe form from a chair and held out his hand. "The clippings are mine," he said quietly.

"And—and may I ask why you are so interested in the Spider?"

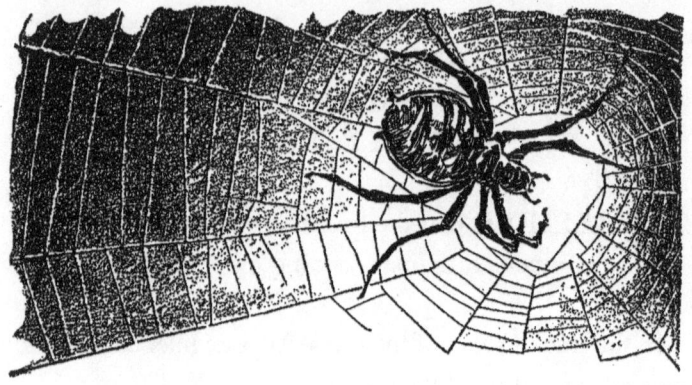

the little man demanded, trying to maintain his importance amid his surprise.

"That is a little matter between the Spider and myself," explained Wentworth unconcernedly as he took the newspaper clippings and passed out to the deck for a constitutional before dressing for dinner…

Two days from New York on the great ocean liner, surrounded by all the comforts and luxury which human ingenuity could devise, a man stood aft on the promenade deck where the glass partition ended. He leaned against the railing and gazed blankly down at the angry swirling waters.

Darkness was falling, and the passengers had left the deck rather deserted. There was a touch of melancholy in the absence of laughter and conversation, in the departing daylight and in the droop of the man's shoulders as he leaned a little dangerously over the railing.

Circling the deck for the last time, Richard Wentworth came

to a sudden halt as he rounded a corner and caught sight of the passenger who stood by the railing. Tall and strongly built, Wentworth's athletic stride ended with such abruptness as to indicate a man whose mind and body worked in perfect unison. Quite motionless, he stood and watched the man at the railing as though he read a message in the drooping shoulders—a message which might have to be answered very quickly.

The man at the railing leaned farther over the sea. He knew nothing of the one who watched him, and only a numbing anticipation of cold waters dwelt in his mind. He did not even feel the pressure of the palms of his hands upon the railing as he raised himself from the deck.

At that last critical second the silent watcher moved with lightning speed across the intervening deck. He grasped the would-be suicide by the collar and jerked him roughly back upon his feet. There was no witness to the rescue.

RAM SINGH, Richard Wentworth's Hindu servant, inserted a tiny cornflower in the lapel of his absent master's dinner coat. He performed the small act with a reverence which would almost indicate a ritual. The florist of every ocean liner carried a supply of these blue flowers when Wentworth crossed.

Ram Singh, expressionless except that his eyes were keen

In one more second Wentworth would have been dead—but an almost
inaudible cough sounded from beneath his handkerchief.

and glittering, surveyed the evening clothes upon the white
bed. Everything was in place.

But Wentworth was a little late.

Ram Singh, bare footed and turbaned, in full Eastern dress,
entered the sitting room of the two-room suite and inspected
the bucket of ice which the steward always brought before

dinner. The ice must be cracked to the right size so that it could be placed in the cocktail shaker at the last moment and a perfect drink produced as the crowning act of dressing his master.

A moment later Richard Wentworth entered with a companion. Ram Singh, inscrutable, stood to one side and noted that his master's companion seemed rather pale and that his collar was torn open in front as though it had been jerked very roughly from behind. At a few words in Hindustani from Wentworth, the servant vanished into the bedroom, leaving the two men alone in the sitting room.

Wentworth turned to the cocktail shaker and began to manipulate the ice and ingredients. "You might tell me about it, Parsons," he said with his back turned.

Parsons threw himself weakly into a chair and hesitated. Then he blurted out the whole story in a very few words. He seemed to be a decent enough man of middle age, but with a chin that was a trifle weak. He was the private secretary of a very wealthy passenger and he had lost, at cards during the voyage, a thousand dollars of his employer's money. Nothing remained for him to do except to go down into the sea and end it all.

"Married?" asked Wentworth, turning suddenly and extending a cocktail.

The wretched man nodded and accepted the glass in a trembling hand, while Wentworth raised his own glass and regarded the color of the liquid with the eyes of a connoisseur. There was a moment's silence.

"Picture?" The question came sharply from Wentworth and

5

RAM SINGH

seemed to carry its full meaning by the actual power of thought.

Parsons took out his pocketbook and extracted a photograph which he handed to Wentworth. It was a snapshot of a sweet-faced woman who stood upon a lawn holding a small terrier in her arms.

Suddenly Wentworth looked more closely at the snapshot. "Hello!" he exclaimed. "What's the matter with the dog's leg?"

"Rather a bad cut," explained Parsons in surprise. "And did a vet place the bandage?"

"No. As a matter of fact I put the bandage on the dog's leg."

Wentworth sipped his drink, placed it upon a table and the trace of a smile flashed upon his lean but rather handsome face as he gazed again at the terrier in the arms of the woman. "You made a pretty good job of it," he commented. "I think I shall repay the dog's debt to you by giving you back your thousand dollars."

"I—I don't understand."

"Dogs are my weakness. You helped a dog; I'll help you."

"You would actually give me a thousand dollars of your money because I placed a bandage on a dog's leg?" asked Parsons in amazement.

"Certainly not," was the quick reply, "but I shall find considerable pleasure in taking your thousand dollars away from the man who rooked you."

Parsons shook his head despondently. "It was fair play."

"No, it was not," contradicted Wentworth. "Not much happens on board a ship that I do not see. You were playing with a very large man named Blunton. He is an expert trans-Atlantic cardsharp. I have studied criminals for years and I know many who are unknown to the police. You had no more chance with Blunton than a child would have if it attempted to strangle a gorilla."

"What a fool I have been!" exclaimed Parsons in a low voice after a pause.

"Any man is a fool who plays cards with strangers," was the dry reply.

"But how can you get my money back?" asked Parsons dubiously. "After all, this man may not have cheated. I really think that he won by superior play. You cannot prove that he cheated. How can you get my money back?"

Richard Wentworth's eyes became a little tense, and the

pupils contracted slightly. There was a touch of exultation upon his face and a fleeting hint of animal ferocity before he spoke. "By right of might," he said in a low voice as if speaking more to himself than to Parsons. "It is a game I love."

HE RETURNED the photograph and rang the bell. "Steward," Wentworth said when the bell was answered, "give Mr. Blunton my compliments and tell him that I would like to see him."

"Very good, sir."

"This man, Blunton," said Wentworth to Parsons when the steward had left, "is one of the scourges of society. During his career he has undoubtedly wrecked the happiness of hundreds of families. Because of him, in all probability, a number of men have committed the act which you attempted. The ordinary man has no chance against him."

In a few minutes the steward returned. "Mr. Blunton says, sir, that he would be glad to see you if you will step over to his stateroom."

"Go back to Mr. Blunton," directed Wentworth, "and tell him that I shall wait here for ten minutes. If he does not arrive in that time, I shall telephone New York, ship to shore service, and discuss his case with the Commissioner of Police."

"Yes, sir," replied the steward, too well trained to show any surprise at the unusual message.

"But have you any legal evidence against the man?" asked Parsons nervously when the steward had departed for the second time.

"Not a shred of legal evidence," admitted Wentworth with

complete indifference. "You see, my dear fellow, I am just making contact with the enemy, pushing a patrol up to his first line to feel him out. I shall come to grips with him a little later."

The steward was a trifle embarrassed when he returned and hesitated in the doorway.

"Begging your pardon, sir, but it's a little awkward."

Wentworth smiled. "Just what is awkward, steward?"

"The message, sir. I don't like to deliver it to you."

Wentworth's smile broadened. "Go ahead, steward. I can stand it if you can."

"Well, sir, Mr. Blunton says that you can go to hell."

"Thank you, steward. That will be all."

Wentworth rose and went into the bedroom, closing the door behind him. Ram Singh, sensing action, stood alert and waiting. Without any words he interpreted a gesture from his master and swiftly dragged forth a riding boot from where it stood beside its mate in a large wardrobe trunk.

"There is plenty of time, Ram Singh," said Wentworth quietly. "We have all night."

But Ram Singh was too earnest to slow his movements. Rapidly he extracted the boot-tree from the shining boot. His nimble fingers sought certain spots, and suddenly the wooden tree fell apart, exposing a considerable cavity. Another moment, and the Hindu picked a peculiar pistol from that cavity and handed it to his master.

Wentworth examined the pistol to make certain that the mechanism was in order. It was one of the most powerful and deadly air pistols that could be constructed and had been especially created for Wentworth by an exceedingly clever engineer—a master mechanic who owed his life to the strange man who now dropped the pistol into his righthand coat pocket.

On top of the pistol Wentworth placed a handkerchief, allowing one corner to protrude slightly from the pocket.

Ram Singh followed his master back into the sitting room and stood beside Parsons.

There was cold determination in Wentworth's simple words before he stepped out into the passage. "I shall expect you both to wait until I return," he said.

Then he was gone.

CHAPTER 2
SEAL OF THE SPIDER

BUT WENTWORTH did not immediately call upon Blunton, the transatlantic gambler. He seldom did what he might be expected to do, something which often rendered him more dangerous to his enemies. For half an hour he stood upon the deck and looked across the dark water, feeling its mysterious influence while the face of a girl came into his mental vision.

It was a delicate face and so vibrant with life that it held the strength of a spring day. Deep blue eyes spoke poetry beneath masses of rich brown curls. Yet there was no lack of worldly experience in those eyes. They had seen life, understood it and were not afraid. In two days Wentworth would see those eyes in reality.

RICHARD WENTWORTH

Reluctantly now he left the rail and turned his mind to the task in hand.

Blunton sat, comfortably bulked, in the largest chair of his suite. Outwardly he was a wealthy passenger who was accustomed to all the luxuries of life. But his face was very hard and displayed innate cruelty as he scowled at the cards which he dealt upon a small table in a game of solitaire.

A few minutes earlier Blunton had declined to enter a game of poker which might have been exceedingly profitable to him. He had declined because a steward had brought him a surprising message which included mention of the Commissioner of Police of New York. He did not like New York's Commissioner of Police, especially when he was about to arrive in New York, and did not wish to have anything to do with him.

Consequently he was playing very safe by remaining in his suite and amusing himself, or trying to amuse himself, by playing solitaire. Certainly there was no law against solitaire.

There was a knock upon the door. Blunton's right hand slipped beneath his dinner coat and paused for a moment beneath his left armpit. There was a slight click as a safety catch was thrown off. It was well to be prepared—in his profession.

"Come in."

The door opened and closed, and Richard Wentworth stood with his back to it as he looked across the little table at the big man with the merciless, poker face.

"And what may I do for you?"

"My name is Wentworth."

"Really? One of the Wentworths of Chicago?"

"I see that your profession has familiarized you with the names of the leading families of America."

Blunton's face remained entirely expressionless as he leaned back in his chair. "Did you come here to insult me?" he asked coldly.

Richard Wentworth drew a handkerchief from the side pocket of his coat. Leisurely he touched it to his nose, partially replaced it in the same pocket and took a chair, uninvited, across the table from Blunton.

"This is serious, Blunton." Wentworth also was very calm,

but his manner was easier, more adroit, than that of Blunton. "I came for the thousand dollars that you took away from Parsons. He couldn't afford to lose it."

"He should not play cards if he cannot afford to lose," returned Blunton indifferently.

"Quite right," agreed Wentworth. "Parsons, however, has a wife and she, too, is going to suffer."

Blunton laughed with the trace of a sneer. "If Parson's wife is unusually good looking, it is just possible that I might make a deal with her."

"Do you never do a kind act, Blunton?"

The big man laughed sarcastically. "You amuse me."

"Well, I am being highly entertained myself," returned Wentworth.

There was a silence while the two men watched each other across the little table. Blunton's eyes had become a little tense. But his expression, if it could be called an expression, was one of determined waiting.

Wentworth's face, in contrast, held considerable mobility, but that mobility placed him at no disadvantage because it gave him the appearance of having nothing to conceal.

"You might as well know at once," said Blunton after the pause, "that I refuse to give you any money at all."

"Too bad!" retorted Wentworth as though he really meant it. "In that case I shall have to *take* the money away from you." BLUNTON BENT forward and regarded his opponent very keenly. Was it possible that his visitor was insane? But there was no insanity in those searching eyes which met his so easily.

"Mr. Wentworth, what is your real reason for interfering in my affairs?" he asked deliberately.

"Mere accident."

"Accident?"

"I happen to be on my way to New York, Blunton," explained Wentworth suavely, "to meet one of the greatest criminals of all times; a man whose nature is so cunning and, at the same time so brutal, that it is a delight to fight him. Compared to him you are a repulsive child, a contemptible cardsharp, who affords me some trifling excitement to break the monotony of this trip."

Blunton was becoming angry. He was losing his temper. "Get out of here before I smash you and throw you out!" he barked savagely.

Wentworth raised a finger from the edge of the table and regarded the spot upon which it had been pressing. Slowly his hand dropped to his right pocket and rose with the large handkerchief. He rubbed the spot carefully and regarded it again.

"You know, Blunton," he said as he again partially replaced the handkerchief in the same pocket, "I don't want any of my finger prints around here in case I am forced to kill you."

Blunton's hand stole a little way beneath his dinner coat.

"I would advise you not to do it," warned Wentworth, "unless you wish to die sooner than may be necessary."

Blunton's hand stopped. He had the feeling of being slowly caught in a web, a sensation which he disliked exceedingly—

although he had, himself, administered it to many of his victims. He resented the feeling so much that his anger increased.

"I shall ring for the steward," he stated slowly, not quite controlling his voice.

"By all means!" Wentworth agreed emphatically. "You will be surprised when you see who answers the bell."

This was pure bluff, but Blunton did not know it or, at least, could not be sure of it. He paused to think while Wentworth picked the cards from the table and arranged them into a pack.

"Cut you for a hundred."

With the gambler's instinct Blunton nodded and cut the cards, a five spot. Wentworth cut and exposed a seven spot. It was pure luck, Wentworth's luck perhaps.

Wentworth held out his right hand, and Blunton drew forth his pocketbook, bulging with money. Wentworth's left hand, the unexpected hand, shot forward and back with lightning speed, and Blunton was left without his pocketbook.

Momentarily stunned, Blunton saw Wentworth's right hand sink to his coat pocket and rise again so that his handkerchief was exposed just above the edge of the table. But Blunton was too hardened a man to be stunned for more than a moment. With incredible speed his hand flashed beneath his coat. His eyes blazed fury, and a black automatic seemed to leap into the air.

IN ONE more second Wentworth would undoubtedly have been dead, but an almost inaudible cough sounded from beneath his handkerchief. The black automatic clattered upon the table. From a hole in Blunton's forehead two drops of blood emerged and struggled downward as far as an eyebrow before the heart ceased beating.

The gambler, who had baffled international police systems, had ended his career.

Wentworth retained his usual calmness, but he moved quickly. A steward, or somebody else, might come to the stateroom at any moment, and time was valuable. Quickly he bolted the door, first pulling on thin, silk gloves so that no finger prints might remain. From the gambler's pocketbook he removed two five-hundred dollar bills and returned the rest of the money to the pocket of the dead man. He performed this act as though it were of very little consequence and instantly became intent upon something of greater importance.

With infinite care, but with incredible rapidity, he began a search of Blunton's clothing and baggage. His agile fingers, thinly covered as they were, touched, moved and left exactly as found everything that the gambler possessed. Not until the very last, when success seemed highly improbable, did he find anything that interested him. Then, returning to the body in the chair, he fingered the shoulder holster which had contained the automatic pistol that still lay upon the table. At the back of the holster was a small flap covering a tiny pocket in the leather, and from this pocket he drew a thin piece of oiled paper.

For a few moments Wentworth scrutinized the fine writing which appeared with a diagram upon the oiled paper. He was looking at a description of the strong room, or bullion room, of a great ocean steamship. The name of the liner appeared at the bottom of the description, and Wentworth knew that the ship in question was even then in mid-ocean with a huge foreign payment to the United States!

Wentworth pocketed the slip of paper and shrugged his shoulders. Blunton was now harmless, but he knew that Blunton had only been the tool of a criminal so dangerous that the police seemed helpless to combat him. That criminal, it would seem, was planning such a crime as would leave the entire world aghast!

Then it was that Wentworth did a dangerous thing. From a cunning artifice, secretly contrived at the bottom of his cigarette lighter, he withdrew a tiny seal and pressed it upon the forehead of the dead man. There, close to the small hole, was clearly depicted, in rich vermilion, the tiny outline of an ugly spider— the mark of the mysterious killer who had shocked New York City at intervals throughout a number of years.

The act seemed more than dangerous. It seemed utterly reckless. Only a man like Richard Wentworth, if there were such another man, would have incurred such a risk.

In a few hours, perhaps in a few minutes, the ship would be agog with excitement. A murder had been committed, and the most baffling criminal of modern times would be known to be on the ship. The news would be flashed to shore and would be the sensation of the morning papers. "The Spider" was coming to New York! Hundreds of the best detectives would meet the boat, and the keenest minds of New York's great police force would study the lives and habits of every person who arrived on the boat.

Even as Wentworth replaced the tiny seal—his death seal if

discovered in his possession—and dropped the cigarette lighter into his pocket, a knock sounded upon the door. Perhaps he had reached the closing scene of his adventurous life. He had only split seconds in which to think and to act.

But most of his life Wentworth had been accustomed to thinking and acting in split seconds. Quickly and silently he unbolted the door, again using his handkerchief to protect his fingers. Then he flattened himself against the wall close to the door and waited. The long fingers of his right hand delicately toyed with the blue flower in his lapel—ready, from that advantageous position, to curve into a fist if he should need to strike.

AGAIN THE knock sounded and, after a brief pause, a steward opened the door and took a few steps into the room. He halted abruptly upon catching sight of the seated man with head sagging gruesomely to one side. The steward's mouth opened in dismay.

Behind him he heard someone else knocking upon the door and turned to see Wentworth apparently entering the room.

"Something wrong?" asked Wentworth, pointing to the man in the chair.

But the steward, a young man, was so upset that he rushed wildly from the room to report his grisly discovery.

Unhurried, Wentworth also left the room, mingled with other passengers and walked out upon the deck where, unnoticed, he dropped the deadly air pistol into the sea. A few minutes later he was at the wireless desk, writing a radiogram to the Commissioner of Police of New York:

ARRIVING WITH THE SPIDER, WHO HAS JUST
PLACED HIS SEAL ON A PROFESSIONAL GAMBLER
STOP FELLOW DESERVED TO BE KILLED BUT THIS
IS YOUR CHANCE TO GET YOUR MAN STOP MEET
THE BOAT WITH THE CREAM OF YOUR DETEC-
TIVES STOP HOPE TO PLAY GOLF WITH YOU NEXT
WEEK...

WENTWORTH

TO PARSONS, when he finally returned to his suite, Wentworth handed the two five-hundred dollar bills.

"I found the fellow dead," he explained, "and was able to take
your money from his pocketbook. There will be an investigation
of course, but there is no need for your employer to learn about
your misconduct—if you do not talk."

The expression on Parson's face was pathetic as his eyes looked
his gratitude. And it was plain to be seen that fear of disgrace
would silence his tongue, even if he should believe that there
was reason for him to talk.

Later that night Wentworth, clad in black pajamas and
propped up by pillows on his bed, held his muted violin to his
chin and played low, throbbing music. Much of the music was
improvised and seemed to express, a longing for something
unobtainable in its mingled sadness and sweetness. Ram Singh
squatted on the floor in the sitting room, his body slightly
swaying with the rhythm of the music. Richard Wentworth
could have been a great musician if he had taken up the violin
professionally.

Abruptly the violinist placed his instrument by his side and took up the hand telephone from the little table by his bed.

"Ship to shore service," he requested and gave a New York City telephone number.

In a remarkably short time, such progress has science made, a feminine voice came across the expanse of ocean, a low, throaty voice, vibrant of life upon a spring day. For a few moments Wentworth spoke in French, the modern language of love, and in his voice was some of the longing of the music he had been playing.

Presently Ram Singh was summoned to the bedroom and, as he had done before on several occasions, held the telephone to his master's ear while the violin was again taken up. Softly Wentworth began to play Kreisler's *Caprice Viennois.* The sweet, haunting music fled from the great, ocean liner to the listening ear in New York. Few women, if any, had ever been wooed in such a way.

Suddenly the captain of the ship, unannounced, stood in the doorway of the bedroom. His face was stern and authoritative as he raised a hand to stop the music, perhaps not quite understanding what Wentworth was doing.

But Wentworth did not stop immediately. Abruptly the soft music changed to one of the most difficult of all violin compositions—*The Devil's Trill* by the immortal Tartini. With the back of his bow Wentworth knocked the mute from the bridge and sent the wild, impetuous music tumbling over itself in throbbing bars of angry, devilish rhythm.

Then the torrent of music ended as abruptly as it had begun.

Wentworth handed the violin to Ram Singh and replaced the telephone without speaking a word.

"I have a wireless about you, Mr. Wentworth, from the Commissioner of Police in New York," stated the captain.

"Yes?" questioned Wentworth indifferently.

"He has asked me to do him the favor," the captain explained, "of having you and all your belongings minutely searched for the seal of the notorious 'Spider.'"

"Yes?" repeated Wentworth with the same indifference. "Hand me my cigarettes and lighter, Ram Singh."

CHAPTER 3
THE BODY ON THE FLOOR

HIGH UP in the tower of Riverside Mansions, in a tiny apartment overlooking the Hudson River, a girl dreamed and worked with a Great Dane for a companion. It was not an expensive apartment, since it could only be reached by climbing stairs from the level where the elevators ended. But it suited Nita van Sloan very well. It suited her purse, and she liked to paint the Palisades at sun-set, and soft, morning lights over the great river.

Sometimes, when mists hung low, blotting out the night lights of Manhattan, she and the huge dog seemed to sleep among the stars.

Apollo, the Great Dane, had been given to Nita when a pup, but he had never forgotten the man who had brought him to the tower apartment and placed his leash in the girl's hand.

Sometimes when the man and girl were together he was still sorely troubled to know upon whose knees he should lay his massive head.

"This is Apollo, the bringer of sudden death," Richard Wentworth had said when he brought the overgrown puppy to the tower apartment…

Now, on a night when mists hung low upon the river, Nita lay asleep in her cubicle among the stars. Stretched upon a window seat the Great Dane also slept, or seemed to sleep. The dog's eyes were closed, but if he slept, he dreamed and not too pleasantly. Deep rumblings, seemingly of disapproval, issued occasionally from him and culminated in a stentorian bark which banished all sleep, or appearance of sleep, from the room.

Nita van Sloan slipped green pajama-clad legs from her bed and crossed the room to sit beside the dog with an arm around his neck. In the soft light of the night, she was extremely pretty, and the dog was very handsome as he lifted his huge head a little to look into her eyes.

"What is it, old boy?" she asked. "Is our Dick in trouble?"

The dog gave a short bark, something he always did at the mention of that name when they were alone together. He left the window seat and crossed the room to return with a riding crop in his mouth. It was Richard Wentworth's riding crop, and the dog placed it across Nita's green-clad knees.

The girl took the crop in her hands and held it tightly. Her deep, blue eyes stared down upon the rolling clouds of mist over the river as if she sought for something beyond human

NITA VAN SLOAN

comprehension. Presently she began to speak her thoughts aloud.

"I can hear music," she said softly. "Somewhere, out in the world, he is playing his violin. He may be in Africa or in India or he may even be in New York City. One never knows, Apollo."

For a long time she sat upon the window seat, as if listening, while Apollo placed his forelegs beside her and his head against her knees... They were interrupted by the ringing of the telephone on the small table beside her bed.

She sped across the room, and the dog followed her alertly as if he knew that things sometimes happened suddenly when that bell sound came very late at night.

She had been thinking so intently about him that his voice came as no surprise. But she crushed the telephone to her ear in fear of missing any sound while she lay upon the bed listening. The dog placed his head near her pillow and she found it and fondled it unconsciously with her free hand.

Richard Wentworth was coming to New York and would arrive in two days. The news thrilled her. It had been six months since she had seen him, and the last time she had heard from him he had telephoned her from Paris to describe a rare piece of Oriental china which he had just bought.

Tonight he was not talking about Oriental china. He was talking to her in a way that a woman loves best, if she is listening to the one man in all the world. And he was speaking in French! Nita knew full well the mood of Dick Wentworth when he told her things in the French language.

"Ma mie," he said, "you are the repetition of a rare perfume mingled with unexpectedness. When the world is dry and dead you are a bubbling brook and, when the world is coarse and mad, you are a limpid pool in a forest glade. The secret reason for life lies in the touch of your lips and the feel of your arms."

He spoke continuously, giving her no chance to reply, as if he were filled with an urge which would not be denied. And through it all there was a wistful sadness in his voice betokening the possibility of menace, even disaster.

"Attendez, ma chère," he continued, "and I shall tell you what may not be expressed in words. I shall talk to you in the language of your soul."

There was a short pause. Then, through the ether and over

the wires came the strains of a violin. Apollo may have heard the sound for he stood up to his full height with his forefeet upon the bed, listening. The girl lay very still, eyes closed.

Softly, with sweet seductiveness, came the strains of *Caprice Viennois*. The huge dog, transfixed, towered above the girl in the green pajamas while, two days from shore, a man played a muted violin and voyaged upon the course of his destiny.

Then came the swift, shocking change.

The sweetness of the haunting music was gone, and in its place was the crashing wildness and the devilish angriness of Tartini's great violin composition, *The Devil's Trill*.

NITA VAN SLOAN opened her eyes in horror while the dog bared his big teeth in anger at the sight of his mistress so upset. Perhaps the dog even caught the message of the angry chords.

The music ended and there was silence. Not another word came from the ship. Nita heard the click of the distant instrument terminating the connection. With a trembling hand she replaced her own telephone.

Nita van Sloan was the only woman in the world who knew the secret of Richard Wentworth—the secret of his cigarette lighter. She also knew the secret of his violin playing and understood how he expressed his feelings and gave play to his emotions by the use of that instrument. It was no exaggeration that he could talk to her when he drew his bow across the strings, so well she knew him.

And now she knew that great danger had suddenly descended upon him while playing *Caprice Viennois*. She knew that he seldom told her when he was in danger. But she believed that, this time, he had had no opportunity to do so. Had his violin music been the automatic expression of his changed state of mind, or had he tried to send her a message—perhaps an appeal for help?

The front door bell sounded as Nita, very much worried and puzzled, sat upon the window seat with the dog.

Apollo lumbered to the door to see what manner of person called upon his mistress so late at night. Nita followed him and opened the door to find a telegraph boy, or what appeared to be a telegraph boy. She took the message. Apollo growled, and the boy ran—the first slight mistake of a great and cunning organization. The boy had not waited to obtain a signature!

GO QUICKLY TO MY APARTMENT AND DESTROY WHAT SHOULD BE DESTROYED.

Nita was completely puzzled. The message appeared to be a radiogram from an incoming ship and was signed "Richard Wentworth," but she knew of nothing in Wentworth's apartment which should be destroyed. Her mind immediately flashed to a certain article, an article she dreaded to think about. But she knew that Wentworth never allowed that article to leave his possession.

Again she read the message, pondering. She thought of something else. On the mantlepiece of Wentworth's music room was an old Ming vase, the rarest piece of Wentworth's collection of Chinese porcelain. In this case, she knew, he had placed some slight fragments of evidence which he had accumulated against a great and mysterious criminal, a man who was planning a crime that would shock the world. But Nita could not believe that Wentworth would wish her to destroy this evidence. It would be the last thing that he would wish destroyed.

Once again she read the message and noticed the signature. Never before had Wentworth sent her any message with a signature other than "Dick."

"Dick didn't send this message, old boy," she said to Apollo, "but we'll have to go just the same. Maybe it's from the Underworld." She paused in thought. "Maybe it's from the police." She patted the dog's head. "Maybe we can do some good."

THE GREAT structure on Park Avenue, where Richard Wentworth lived when in town, was always fully staffed, day and night. And Nita was in some doubt regarding her ability to obtain admission to his rooms. She knew that it was practically an impossibility for a young woman to ascend, unannounced, in one of the elevators if she were not well known. She had a key to the apartment and power of attorney to act for Wentworth in his absence. But well trained servants might easily refuse to act upon a legal document until it had been passed upon by the agents of the building on the following day.

Nita entered this perfectly conducted building with some apprehension, although she held her head high and crossed the hall as though she had every right to do so.

To her intense surprise a stiff hall man bowed her in the direction of an elevator.

"Mistaken for somebody else," thought Nita and stepped into the elevator followed by Apollo.

Without any question the elevator man shot the car up to the floor she named. Nita noticed that his uniform did not seem to fit him very well. And as she stepped out of the elevator she decided that something was decidedly wrong. Things were being made altogether too easy for her.

The elevator descended and left Nita and the dog in a private hall outside the apartment of Richard Wentworth. Nita took a key from her handbag. She shrugged her shoulders and remarked to the dog:

"Old boy, we are in for it. Somebody is bungling it, and we are evidently expected. At least I am expected; perhaps you will be the joker in the deal."

Apollo lifted a paw and put it in a bowl of roses on a small table which faced the elevator in the private hall. Apollo liked the feel of water on his paw. The bowl of roses went to the floor with a crash.

"Ssh!" warned Nita, but smiled while Apollo looked the other way as if he did not see what he had done. "They know we're coming. Why tell 'em?"

The great dog rose on his hind legs, so that his head was higher than hers, and placed his forepaws upon her shoulders. This was his way of expressing adoration. She did not mind his wet paws.

"It's the Underworld or the police on the other side of that door," she said, looking into the dog's eyes, "but it's for Dick, our Dick."

The name she mentioned brought a deep, short bark from

the dog. He lowered himself to the floor and placed a paw against the door before she could use her key.

The door swung open easily upon complete blackness.

NOT MANY young women would have entered an unlighted apartment under such uncertain conditions. Not many young women, however, are accompanied by such a dog as Apollo. And Nita was one of the Van Sloans who had come to America before the revolution, and courage had always lived in her family—courage and the spirit of adventure. The Van Sloan courage had been with her father when he died in the War.

Her pride of family and her spirit of adventure carried her into the dark apartment.

But she did remove Apollo's muzzle and slip the leash from his collar. "Might as well be ready, old boy," she said.

The dog surged ahead into the darkness. He knew that apartment, and he knew who lived in it. It smelled very good to him in the darkness as he stopped to sniff. A dog's nose leads to his heart.

Nita found the electric switch and illuminated the hall of the apartment. It was a large hall and indicated a very luxurious establishment. The white covered furniture seemed rather ghostly. Only a large Ming vase of aubergine enamel was uncovered. It stood upon a high pedestal, and Nita was rather surprised to notice that its covering was lying upon the floor at the base of the pedestal. Then she heard the dog growling in another room.

"Apollo!"

The growls ceased and the dog's feet were audible on the

polished floor as he answered her call. He appeared from a dark doorway and looked at her. Evidently he had found something which displeased him but did not really anger him and certainly did not frighten him.

"What is it, old boy?" she asked, moving toward him.

The dog turned and disappeared into the room from which he had emerged. It was Wentworth's music room, and Nita knew that it contained the rarest of the Oriental china. She advanced to the dark doorway and tried to look in. But she could see nothing, and it was evident that the heavy blinds had been completely drawn. Again the dog began to growl, deep guttural sounds of disapproval.

Nita reached a hand into the dark room, feeling for the electric switch. As she did so there was a click from behind her, and the hall was thrown into darkness. Desperately she turned toward the partially open front door, the door she had not quite closed when she entered the apartment.

A man was in the act of leaving the apartment. He seemed to be carrying something, and the outside light fell upon his face for one fleeting second before the front door closed and all the apartment was blank darkness.

Nita van Sloan needed all her courage in that brief second. The face she had seen was cruel and repulsive, like the face of a man who gloated over some terrible act, *but it seemed to be the face of Richard Wentworth!*

Under the shock of what she had seen, her trembling knees carried her a few paces from the doorway of the music room before she sank upon the polished floor in the dark, a small heap of misery and fear. She did not faint, but she gave a little cry of mental anguish.

In the music room Apollo heard that little cry and the scratching of his nails upon the hard floor told of his eagerness to reach her. In his reckless progress he struck a chair and sent it crashing against the wall. Then he was with her, ears and nose guiding him in the blackness. For quite awhile she sat upon the floor with her arm around the great dog's neck.

"It can't be true," she whispered over and over again. "He *couldn't* look like that!"

The dog crouched close beside her and rubbed his head against hers. Not sensing an enemy, there was nothing else that he could do.

Presently she rose to her feet and, holding tight to the back of Apollo's neck where the skin was loose, searched until she found the light-switch in the hall. She opened the front door, but there was no one in the private entrance by the elevator shaft.

With the light again shining upon the shrouded furniture and the great Ming vase, Nita realized that the departing man must have come from the dining room or from the passage leading to the bedrooms. She shivered as she thought of the face she had seen, but turned resolutely toward the music room.

"Come on, Apollo," she said. "We'll see what you have been doing all the growling about."

The dog seemed to understand her and went swiftly back into the room he had left. He was again growling in the darkness when she found the electric switch and flooded the music room with light.

What Nita van Sloan saw under the flood of light in the music room was far more horrible than what she had seen in that fleeting second at the front door. There, upon the floor in contorted attitude, and evidently quite dead, lay a man. His face was hideous and the manner of his death was plain to be seen. Around his neck was a silk cord, drawn cruelly tight and knotted.

Apollo ceased his growling and looked up at Nita as if to know what was to be done.

CHAPTER 4
SPIDER BAIT

THIS TIME Nita did not tremble or sink to the floor. She looked away, as was natural, from so horrible a sight and walked slowly back into the hall, thinking very hard. She was concerned not with the dead man upon the floor but about the man at the front door. Had it really been her Dick? Was it possible for him to look like the devil she had seen? Had he really telephoned her from a ship at sea? Who had so vilely murdered the man in the music room?

Apollo stood beside her in the hall. Having shown her what he had found, he was careless of what lay behind him in the music room. She looked down at him and wished he had seen the face at the door. *He* would have known. Then she was ashamed of herself. Dick Wentworth could never express such cruelty as she had seen, could never be connected with anything so horrible as the thing in the music room. It was the one fear which had held her back. She took up a telephone.

"Give me the Police Department, please." Her voice was cool and her hand did not shake as she held the telephone. There was a very brief wait. "There has been a murder at the apartment of Richard Wentworth." She heard a voice ordering radio cars to the address on Park Avenue almost as she gave it.

"Who are you?" a voice demanded.

Concealment was impossible; she could never escape the investigation which must follow. "Miss Nita van Sloan," she answered calmly.

"What are you doing at Mr. Wentworth's apartment at this time of night?"

Nita hung up the telephone. She would have to answer questions sooner or later, but she wanted time to think. What would she say? What *could* she say?

With Apollo closely accompanying her she walked into Wentworth's bedroom and looked at the framed picture of herself which hung upon the wall at the foot of his bed. As she turned to leave she noticed some wrapping paper and twine in disorderly array upon the counterpane.

In a remarkably few minutes the first radio car arrived and two uniformed men ascended to the Wentworth apartment. A single look at the dead man was enough to cause one of them to jump for the telephone. The murdered man had been a plainclothesman, one of the smartest detectives of the New York Police Department.

The two policemen turned on Nita with harsh, swift, penetrating questions.

Nita remained silent. The policemen put their questions more brutally and in louder voices. Apollo growled savagely and crouched for a spring. The policemen drew their night sticks. Nita threw her arms around the Great Dane's neck and held him back just as the telephone rang.

A few words over the telephone worked a miracle in the attitude of the policemen. The one at the telephone whispered to his companion before approaching Nita and apologized to her. Would she forgive them? They had only been trying to do their duty. Mr. Stanley Kirkpatrick, the Commissioner of Police himself, had telephoned her his compliments, together with his hopes that she would

be kind enough to wait until he arrived so that he could relieve her of any unpleasantness.

Nita settled herself in a comfortable chair and Apollo stretched himself at her feet at her command. She knew that Kirkpatrick was almost as astute as Wentworth himself, and she realized that she was waiting for an exceedingly searching examination, no matter how politely the Commissioner might conduct himself.

More uniformed men arrived. Plainclothesmen came. Finger-print men and photographers brought their apparatus. The rooms soon became filled with men at work upon their cunning

The face she had seen was cruel and repulsive—like the face of a man who gloated over some cruel and terrible act.

profession. Two lieutenants arrived and finally a captain came and took charge. Yet not one of them bothered Nita or asked her any questions, except the captain, who wanted to know if she was quite comfortable.

Then the Commissioner of Police arrived with an inspector. **NITA KNEW** Stanley Kirkpatrick, the Commissioner of Police, personally. He was one of New York's few society commissioners but, notwithstanding, was one of the shrewdest men ever to command the Police Force.

In the dining room, alone with Kirkpatrick, Nita told her story very simply. She told him everything except about her telephone conversation with Wentworth and about the face she had seen at the door.

"I knew that the telegram was not genuine," she explained, "but Dick Wentworth and I are such old friends that I felt it my duty to see if anything was wrong at his apartment."

"Rather dangerous, wasn't it?"

"There was Apollo."

"Ah, yes, of course!" The Commissioner stroked the dog's head for a moment. "Miss Van Sloan, I shall just get a report from my men, and then I shall have something to tell you. After that, if you will be so good as to permit me, I shall drive you home."

"Then you are not going to arrest Apollo and me and do all kinds of horrid things to us?" she asked smiling.

The Commissioner laughed pleasantly. "Neither one of you is capable of strangling one of my best detectives, and Dick

Wentworth would never forgive me if I permitted you to be annoyed."

When he returned to the dining room he asked her quickly if she had seen anybody else in the apartment before the first policeman had arrived.

She shook her head, not willing to speak of the resemblance between Wentworth and the man she had seen at the door for the brief second. But his keen eyes were watching her, and she knew that she had not deceived him.

"Very well," he continued as if it did not matter. "Now let me tell you something. Wentworth has been in Europe in search of one of the cleverest and most ruthless of criminals, a strangler who escaped from New York after completely baffling my entire force. The strength of this criminal lies in his astounding ability to impersonate other people."

"Impersonate other people!" exclaimed Nita.

"Yes," said the Commissioner. "You saw him here tonight, but you were afraid to tell me, fearing that it might actually be Dick Wentworth himself."

Nita controlled her face wonderfully. But she knew that her sudden relief did not escape her astute companion. However, her heart was singing again and she was ready, or thought she was ready, for anything that might follow.

"This great criminal," continued Kirkpatrick, "escaped from Wentworth and returned to New York ahead of him. Tonight he actually impersonated Richard Wentworth before the hall servants and came up to this apartment where he met one of my detectives and murdered him. Why he came here I do not know."

"But what was your detective doing here?" asked Nita.

"That has to do with another great criminal, the 'Spider.'"

"The Spider?" she asked and appeared very puzzled.

"Dick Wentworth," he said, "is returning to New York on a ship which the notorious Spider has just made another killing."

"Well?" she questioned.

"Most of my detective force," the Commissioner continued, "is at work upon the Spider case and is preparing to meet the ship when it arrives." He paused and looked at her as if a little undecided. "Up to the present moment I know of only one man on that ship who was present in New York when the other Spider crimes took place. That man is Dick Wentworth."

NITA FOUGHT to quiet the quickened beating of her heart. "And Dick's friend could think of that?" She asked with every appearance of disdain.

This time she felt certain that he did not penetrate her thoughts. He moved a trifle uncomfortably and looked down under the disdain in her eyes.

"It is just because I *am* his friend," he insisted, "and because I knew what he would have done in my place that I had to prove him innocent to my own satisfaction. Dick Wentworth is the cleverest man I know, and I want to work with him again as I have in the past even if he does sometimes make my force seem ridiculous when we blunder. I must know him to be innocent or—" He paused and then looked straight into her eyes.

"Have you ever noticed that the Spider has never harmed a decent man?"

There was still some disdain in her eyes, although it had softened. "And have you proved him innocent?" she asked.

"Not—yet."

She looked her question.

"I knew you to be Dick Wentworth's closest friend," he continued, "and I had one of my detectives send you the bogus radiogram while he hid in this apartment to see if you would reveal the hiding place of anything incriminating. He succeeded in discovering the greatest of all secrets—death."

Some of the disdain crept back into her eyes. "And is that all that you have done?"

The Commissioner shook his head. "I have done more," he continued. "I sent a radiogram to the captain of the ship asking him to subject Wentworth and all his belongings to a minute inspection in search of the tiny Spider seal which is used to mark all of the 'Spider's' work. It is a British ship, and a very good Scotland Yard man is on board. A very rigid inspection was made."

Her question came almost saucily. "Well, did you find any spiders?"

"Not a spider."

"Well?"

"However, I have had a very long radiogram from the Scotland Yard man," the Commissioner continued, "and I find that there was a slight carelessness in the search which he made. When Wentworth was told that he was to be searched he asked

Wentworth had her in his arms before the fragments of the vase ceased trembling.

for his cigarettes and cigarette lighter and did not seem in the least worried. That cigarette lighter was the only article in Wentworth's possession which was not examined, and it is quite large enough to contain the seal of the Spider."

Nita laughed and took cigarettes and cigarette lighter from her handbag. "Like to examine my lighter?" she asked as she delicately lighted a cigarette. "It happens to be a duplicate of the one which Dick Wentworth carries."

Commissioner Kirkpatrick waved the lighter aside. "There is one more test to which I am going to subject Richard Wentworth," he said.

"And that is?"

"I dare not radio back to the ship to have his lighter examined," the Commissioner replied. "If he is guilty, he is too clever to be caught twice in the same way."

"It seems to me that you haven't caught him the first time yet," Nita retorted, smiling through her cigarette smoke.

"True!" admitted Kirkpatrick emphatically. "And I sincerely hope that he is innocent and cannot be caught at all. However, I am going to take him unawares once again. He is flying ashore with the mails and will reach this apartment tomorrow afternoon."

There was an indifferent "Yes?" to this statement.

"In the meantime," he continued, "I have made it impossible for you to communicate with him by the courtesy of a British captain to an American Police Commissioner. I want you to meet him in the hall of this apartment as soon as he comes through the front door."

41

Nita sat up rather straight in her chair, surprised. "Why?" she shot at him quickly.

"As soon as he comes through the door," he explained, "I want you to tell him that the police are here and ask him to give you his cigarette lighter so that you can get rid of it. Speak to him in as low a voice as possible. I shall be where I can see, and a very sensitive microphone will carry the slightest sound to me."

She was gripping an arm of her chair under a fold of her dress, but she laughed. "And if I refuse?"

"In that case," he said, "I shall know what I am trying to discover."

She laughed again and asked: "Why don't you ask him for his lighter yourself?"

Police Commissioner Kirkpatrick stood up and looked gravely down at her before earnestly stating: "Because Richard Wentworth is so damned clever that I am afraid of him. Because you are the only person in the world who can deceive him."

She laughed again, but her finger nails were biting into the palm of her clenched hand and there was blood on her tiny handkerchief when the Commissioner drove her home to Riverside Mansions, as the mists were lifting from the Hudson River at break of day.

CHAPTER 5
THE CIGARETTE LIGHTER

I N A few minutes Richard Wentworth would open the door of his Park Avenue apartment and face one of the great crises of his life. And he would face that crisis totally unprepared and unwarned! Clever as he was, it seemed that this time there could be no escape.

Nita van Sloan sat in the large hall of the Wentworth apartment, on the following afternoon, and faced the door, waiting. On its high pedestal, towering above her head and close to her chair, was the big Chinese vase of aubergine enamel. At her feet Apollo slept, or appeared to sleep. A slender leash connected the dog's collar with her small hand.

There were no members of the New York Police Department in the hall where she sat and no trace of them. There were, however, a number of detectives and some uniformed men still at work in the interior rooms. And the Police Commissioner, himself, stood in a doorway behind some portiers in such a way that he could see the front door.

A head-clamp held a transmitter to one of his ears—a transmitter that was connected with a concealed microphone which would amplify the slightest whisper which might be uttered in the hall where Nita sat.

Nita knew that she could not warn Wentworth by a single, whispered word, without revealing his fatal secret to the listening ear of the Commissioner. She could make no warning sign that his eye would not see. Unbelievably clever as she knew

43

Dick Wentworth to be, she did not think it possible for him, under such conditions, to destroy the convicting evidence which was concealed in the cigarette lighter which he always carried. Before Commissioner Kirkpatrick she had maintained a humorous attitude with just a touch of disdain. Now she nerved herself for one desperate effort at the last moment.

Could she do it? She didn't know.

A detective telephoned that Wentworth had left the landing field and was traveling uptown by taxi with his Hindu servant, that he would arrive in about fifteen minutes. The Commissioner of Police took off his head-phones and Nita carelessly dropped Apollo's leash at the base of the pedestal upon which stood the Chinese vase.

"Care for a cigarette?" the Commissioner asked, coming into the hall.

Nita took the cigarette but refused his match. "I shall light it with Dick Wentworth's lighter," she said, "after you have apologized to him."

Presently the Commissioner went back behind the portiers and Nita idly picked up the leash. In doing so she reached behind the pedestal and drew the cord around its base before hitching the end about the leg of her heavy chair.

In a few minutes there was the sound of a latch key. The door opened and Richard Wentworth stepped into the hall followed by Ram Singh...

WHAT HAPPENED then happened swiftly. Apollo looked up, rose and surged toward the man he loved. The light leash, circling the pedestal, went taut and snapped under his great weight. The pedestal rocked, and the heavy vase slipped from its resting place. Nita, half rising from her chair, caught the full weight of the vase on the top of her head as it fell.

Her knees gave way beneath her and she collapsed upon the floor, still and inert, while the chrysanthemum-decorated vase smashed into a hundred fragments beside her.

Wentworth sprang forward and had her in his arms before the fragments of the vase had ceased trembling upon the floor. As her head rested against his shoulder, blood trickled from beneath the rich, brown curls and ran across her pale face.

"*Pani lao!*" he snapped at Ram Singh. "*Juldi kuro!*"

While Ram Singh ran to the kitchen for water as ordered, Wentworth carried Nita into the music room and placed her gently upon a lounge. He was touching her bloody face delicately with his handkerchief and testing her pulse with his other hand when Commissioner Kirkpatrick approached him.

"Kirkpatrick," he said after a glance over his shoulder, "for your own sake I hope you are not responsible for this."

"Really, Wentworth!" Kirkpatrick protested. "I would not have had it happen for anything!"

"Then why the devil did you *let* it happen?" retorted Wentworth hotly while he gently tried to find the wound under the brown curls.

"You are not quite fair," the Commissioner continued to protest as Ram Singh came running with a basin of water and towels. "There has been a murder in your apartment."

"I read about it in the afternoon papers," remarked Wentworth as he worked on Nita's face and forehead with a damp towel, "and I notice that you haven't caught the murderer."

"We are doing our best and will get him if it takes a year."

The accident to Nita had angered Wentworth as nothing else could have done. He frowned over his shoulder at Commissioner Kirkpatrick. "You and your whole force," he said coldly, "couldn't catch a jack-rabbit in a ten acre field with a wall around it."

"Just a minute, Wentworth!" exclaimed Kirkpatrick, showing anger himself. "You have no right to be furious with me because I had you searched on board ship." He paused as Nita's eyes began to flutter open. "I simply had to take that action."

The fluttering of Nita's eyelid's seemed to banish all anger from Wentworth. He rose and faced the Commissioner calmly. "It was one of the cleverest things you ever did, but—it didn't get you anywhere."

"No, Wentworth, it didn't," Kirkpatrick replied gravely. "There was one thing which the Scotland Yard man failed to examine and that one thing is just big enough to conceal the Spider's seal. Let me have a look at your cigarette lighter, please!"

RICHARD WENTWORTH smiled condescendingly at the cleverest Commissioner of Police that New York had ever had. The expression of his face was devoid of all fear as he glanced down again at the lounge where Nita was stirring slightly. But the scar of an old wound began to show as a white line across his right temple. Normally invisible, that scar was the only thing about himself which he could not always control in moments of great stress, moments of anger or adversity.

"Really, Kirkpatrick," he said, thinking and rejecting plan after plan as the seconds fled, "will nothing ever satisfy you?"

"Yes, Wentworth, the cigarette lighter."

One last resort came into Wentworth's mind, a poor resort and a humiliating one. He had money in Europe—if he could get there. He glanced casually toward the door of the music room. A policeman stood in the doorway. The New York police force was at work under the guidance of a very clever man.

"And if I refuse?" Wentworth grinned amiably, but the scar was still in evidence, although it was not noticed by the Commissioner, who knew nothing of its import.

The Commissioner shrugged his shoulders, his face grave.

"You would use force?"

Again the Commissioner, silent, shrugged his shoulders, looking gravely at the smiling man.

It was only a matter of seconds, but Wentworth could think many things in a few seconds. It might be possible, barely possible, for him to fight his way out. But fighting would probably mean killing, and he had never killed a policeman. And there was Ram Singh to think about. Ram Singh hovering at one side of the room and already suspicious of trouble.

Ram Singh would certainly fight if any fighting commenced and, when Ram Singh fought, Ram Singh killed. Wentworth was as loyal to his servant as his servant was to him. He could not send the Hindu to Sing Sing or to the electric chair.

"I am waiting, Wentworth." Commissioner Kirkpatrick looked very obstinate and very uncomfortable.

Slowly Wentworth's fingers dipped into a pocket of his vest.

They emerged, cigarette lighter between thumb and forefinger. He handed the lighter to his inquisitor, the smile dying a trifle upon his face.

The Commissioner of Police silently carried the cigarette lighter to a window where he could examine it in a strong light. He stood close to the window scrutinizing the little article intently.

A telephone bell sounded faintly, and Wentworth strolled carelessly to a small cabinet, opened it and picked up the telephone receiver.

"Yes, I am Richard Wentworth," he said in reply to a woman's question, while he watched Kirkpatrick's back at the window. After a pause:"Kill yourself? Oh, I wouldn't do that. How did you know I had returned from Europe?" Another pause. "Didn't know I had been away?" Pause. "Yes, I worked on that case with the New York police before I went to Europe. In fact I have been working on it indirectly for the last few months."

While Wentworth listened for a few moments Kirkpatrick continued to examine the little lighter very minutely. Ram Singh squatted upon the floor, regarding his master with glittering, questioning eyes. The policeman stood motionless in the doorway.

WENTWORTH CONTINUED at the telephone: "Please be calm and speak slowly, my dear lady, and remember that you have not told me who you are." In the silence, while he listened, he seemed to be as calm as if he had a whole life of activity stretching before him—but his eyes never left the Commissioner's back.

"Dorothy Canfield! Of course I remember your name in the case. Your fiancée escaped from the police and has been hunted ever since." Pause. "Tut, tut! Don't think of doing such a thing. Come and see me. There is always a way out."

He replaced the telephone. But was there always a way out? Was not the girl's desperate threat his own best remedy, his only remedy?

Suddenly the Police Commissioner turned with his back to the window. He extended the cigarette lighter to Wentworth, looking very uncomfortable but forcing a smile.

Wentworth took the lighter indifferently and examined it with what appeared to be mock seriousness. Although no trace of surprise was shown upon his face he could scarcely believe what he saw. At its base the little cigarette lighter had no secret repository cleverly contrived by a master mechanic.

It was not his lighter!

"What, no spiders today, Mr. Policeman?" demanded Wentworth jocularly.

Cleverly, when it dawned upon him, he covered his surprise with mock surprise.

"Will somebody give me a light, please?" rather a weak voice asked.

Both men turned sharply toward the lounge, Kirkpatrick still standing with his back to the window.

Nita van Sloan was sitting up on the lounge, a rather crumpled cigarette in her hand. Wentworth snapped the lighter in his hand and held it to her cigarette.

It was then that Commissioner Kirkpatrick carried out his

promise. "I apologize fully and humbly, Wentworth," he said simply.

"But why?" asked Wentworth indifferently while he looked down at Nita far from indifferently. "I might have half a dozen lighters in various pockets, you know."

"No!" denied the Commissioner confidently. "You only had one lighter on board ship and my men gave you no chance to obtain another after you came ashore. Will you accept my apology?"

There was a sharp crack of breaking glass, and the Police Commissioner swayed away from the window and fell, unconscious to the floor before Wentworth, quick as he was, could catch him!

Through the plate glass of the window a bullet hole showed. In half a minute the room was full of policemen, busy upon what seemed to be another case of murder!

Amid the confusion Richard Wentworth knelt beside the lounge with his lips very close to Nita's ear. "You were never unconscious," he whispered. "You took it out of my pocket and substituted yours while I carried you. You wonderful girl!"

She smiled faintly, dropped her cigarette to the floor and rested her aching head upon a pillow, careless of what he was or what he did so long as he was safe.

Ram Singh, amid the turmoil, solemnly removed his shoes and began to wind a long turban around his head. In New York streets he dressed according to American custom; but, in his master's home, he rendered his master Oriental service.

CHAPTER 6
ANOTHER WHO
WISHED TO DIE

THE BRAINS of the New York Police Department concentrated upon the great Park Avenue apartment house, concentrated in all its strength and with astonishing celerity.

Seldom had that department been so agitated. Radio cars wove their way inquisitively through traffic in the vicinity. Scores of police, in uniform and in plain clothes, infested the neighborhood for blocks around the building.

Inside the apartment of Richard Wentworth more detectives swarmed. Inspectors almost lost their calm demeanor as they barked sharp orders and, with serious countenances, listened to the reports of experts of ballistics who examined the bullet hole in the window and gazed toward distant roofs and windows, trying to determine the point from which the bullet must have been fired.

Police surgeons came, their sirens screaming a path through New York traffic. They hurried to a bedroom where Stanley Kirkpatrick, Commissioner of Police, lay unconscious, critically ill, probably dying. Shortly they came out to order complete silence in the apartment, to telephone for day and night nurses, for oxygen tanks and for many other things. A great specialist in head wounds was summoned. He came, examined the patient and shook his head. There was a fighting chance for life, he said—provided the patient was not moved from the apartment.

Richard Wentworth sat beside Nita on the lounge in the music room, talking to her in a low voice as calmly as if no such tense excitement surrounded them. In that crowded apartment, large as it was, there was no place in which they could be alone together. As the great specialist was leaving, Wentworth beckoned to him and pointed to Nita's head.

The specialist made a swift examination. "A painful scalp wound," he stated. "I can stitch it under a local anesthetic in a few minutes."

"If you will clear some policemen out of a bedroom," Wentworth suggested, "she can lie down and be comfortable while you do it." He seemed to fumble for a match to light a cigarette as Nita rose. "Lend me your lighter, Nita?" he asked. "You won't be needing it for a few minutes."

The doctor did not see, nor did anybody else notice the flash of fear which came into the girl's blue eyes as she unclenched a hand and handed a cigarette lighter to Wentworth.

As Nita left the music room with the specialist, Wentworth snapped the lighter into action and lit his cigarette. He held the lighter high before his face and examined it critically before extinguishing the light. Near its base, scarcely discernible, was the faint line of demarcation, the secret junction wrought so cunningly by the master mechanic.

SUDDENLY WENTWORTH turned to a nearby inspector and emphasized his words by tapping that inspector on the shoulder with the lighter which he held in his hand. "The man who shot the Commissioner," he said, "is the man I was hunting in Paris, the man who eluded me and returned to New

York ahead of me, the man who strangled your detective here last night."

"But why did he come here last night?" questioned the inspector. "What was his motive?"

"Theft."

"Theft of what?"

"Do you see that pair of mazarine blues, decorated in *famille rose* enamel?"

The inspector followed Wentworth's gaze. "You mean the two Chinese jars on the mantelpiece?"

Wentworth nodded and returned the lighter to his pocket. "Between those two jars you will probably discover that the surface of the mantelpiece shows the faint outline of a ring, indicating that a *third* vase once stood there."

The inspector examined the surface of the mantelpiece and confirmed what Wentworth had suggested.

"The missing vase," Wentworth continued, "is a very rare piece of reticulated porcelain from the Ming period. I believe that the thief, impersonating a waiter in a Paris hotel, overheard me speak to my native servant regarding certain evidence against him which I had left in that vase—a bit of his hair and the imprint of his front teeth on an apple. He beat me back to New York and destroyed that evidence, stealing the vase out of pure hatred for me. It's quite simple, my dear inspector."

"Simple!" exclaimed the inspector. "Who is the thief? Where is he? Why did he shoot the Commissioner of Police after he got away with the jar?"

"I do not know where the thief is," replied Wentworth, "but

he impersonated me and therefore must be a man of about my height, weight and color of eyes."

"Yes," said the inspector, looking into Wentworth's gray-blue eyes and mentally noting his height as five feet eleven inches and his weight as a hundred and seventy pounds, "but why did the criminal hang around and shoot the Commissioner?"

"He didn't intend to shoot the Commissioner."

"No?"

"He thought that he was shooting me. You will notice that I was wearing a suit of clothes which is very similar in color and design to that which was worn by the Commissioner when he was shot. You will also remember that the Commissioner was standing with his *back* to the window when he was shot."

"Oh!" The inspector paused thoughtfully. "And why is this master criminal so intent upon snuffing you out?"

"He knows," answered Wentworth, "that he *must* kill me in order to go on living himself, that sooner or later I shall get him if he does not get me. I believe that he is planning a stupendous crime and that he is afraid I shall block it if he does not kill me."

"What kind of a crime?" demanded the inspector eagerly.

Wentworth shook his head. "My information is so vague at present," he returned, "that you could not appreciate its significance. But I believe that this criminal must be captured or killed if the whole world is not to stand aghast."

A telephone mechanic was busy bringing in a trunk line for police use, and Wentworth picked up his own telephone which, for the moment, was silent. He called a very select employment agency. "Send me a chef," he said, "a butler and enough maids for a fifteen-room apartment." Then he added: "All the servants must have brown eyes."

"Not taking any chance of this fiend coming up here as one of your servants and sticking a knife into you, eh?" remarked the inspector.

"No," said Wentworth. "I scarcely think that this man can change his eyes to brown."

"And the maids? Surely you don't have to be careful about women!"

"You would be surprised!" Wentworth grinned. "He makes up as a woman so well that you could never guess it in a close up."

Ram Singh, silent upon bare feet and with great turban gleaming white, came to Wentworth's side and spoke in a low voice. "Professor sahib!" he said. "Him wait in library. No like police. Not talk."

OLD PROFESSOR BROWNLEE was sitting quietly in the library when Wentworth entered. His eyes lighted up with affection at sight of the younger man, and the grasp of his hand was very warm as they sat down together, alone in the room for the moment.

Years before, when Wentworth was a young man and little more than a boy at college, Professor Brownlee, at that time a professor of physics, had made the great and only mistake of his life. He had misused funds which were in his hands for safekeeping. Wentworth had come to his assistance and, by a clever subterfuge, had saved the professor from criminal proceedings, though he had been unable to prevent him from losing his professorship. The friendship between the two had developed as the years passed.

Fifty miles up the Hudson River, near Cold Spring, Professor Brownlee now maintained a small private laboratory where he experimented and where he performed some miracles of science for Richard Wentworth.

"I got your telegram," the Professor said, "and came as fast as I could."

"It's another air pistol," Wentworth said. "I had to discard the one I had, and I must have another as soon as possible."

"Will tonight do?" Professor Brownlee asked. "I have one already made and I can bring it to you before midnight."

"Good man!" exclaimed Wentworth.

In low voices they continued to talk, and Wentworth exposed his real reason for sending for the Professor. He wanted a new cigarette lighter that would utterly prevent the dangerous seal from being discovered, even if the lighter were taken away from him or lost. Wentworth was determined not to give up the identifying mark which was so dangerous to him. He would, in the meantime, not even cease the use of the lighter which had so nearly destroyed him.

It seemed that he loved the hazard of battling with his wits against the wits of almost all the world, good and bad. In addition, of course, the continuous use of the identical mark permitted him to strike terror into the hearts of his enemies.

"It is a case of the time element," the professor stated. "I could make you a contrivance which would destroy the seal if it fell into anybody else's hands, but it might not do so quickly enough to render detection impossible."

"It must destroy the seal instantaneously," insisted Wentworth, "and the contrivance must be such that it will give no indication that the seal had ever been contained by it."

"That, my friend, is a hard problem and I shall have to sleep over it," Professor Brownlee remarked gravely.

Outside the library there was a slight disturbance, unusual in that place of subdued voices and muffled footfalls. The disturbance increased, and Ram Singh burst into the room, followed by two policemen who were trying to detain him without causing so much noise as to be dangerous to the Commissioner.

Ram Singh fled to his master, an envelope in his hand.

"Sahib!" exclaimed Ram Singh. "Messenger boy come with *chit*. Police *wallahs* try take *chit*. No can do!"

Wentworth took the envelope from the Hindu and looked at the inspector who had entered behind the policemen and with whom he had been talking a few minutes previously.

"If the police interfere with my private life too much," Wentworth remarked a bit acidly, "I shall ask them to go and find some other quarters."

"I am sorry," the inspector apologized. "This is a very serious case and we are all on our toes."

"Toes can be stepped on," said Wentworth sharply and smiled, instantly changing to his very attractive self. "Come over here, inspector, and let's see what the messenger boy has brought me. It looks like a note from a lady."

Wentworth tore the envelope open, read the message and handed it to the inspector with an expressionless face.

The note was addressed to Richard Wentworth and read:

I have potassium cyanide tablets beside me and intend to take them at ten o'clock tonight if you do not come to my assistance before then. You are the one man in all the world who might be able to help me, though I do not know how you can do it. Please do not send a policeman as I shall swallow the tablets if one comes near me. If you come to see me, bring a pistol for your own protection.

At the bottom of the note was the signature, or what appeared to be the signature, of Dorothy Canfield. The handwriting was well formed and indicated a person who was alert and strong minded.

"What do you think of it?" asked Wentworth as the inspector finished reading.

"Judged by the handwriting," the inspector replied, "the writer is in earnest. The address is a side street on the west side of Manhattan. Shall I send a couple of men over to see what it's all about?"

"Better let me go alone," Wentworth disagreed. "She doesn't seem very fond of the police."

"We are mixed up with a very dangerous criminal," said the inspector. "Considering what you have told me about him, don't you think that this message might be a plant—to rub you out?"

"Yes, I have thought of that, said Wentworth. But there was

no trace of concern in face or manner as he began the simple preparations for his departure.

CHAPTER 7
THE MAN IN THE MASK

I T WAS after dark when Richard Wentworth, in evening clothes and with opera hat seated upon his head at a slight angle, strolled out upon Park Avenue and raised his slender cane to stop a passing taxi.

"Take the cutting across Central Park at 86th Street," Wentworth directed the taxi driver, "and let me out at Columbus Avenue."

Wentworth knew his New York very well and he leaned back lazily, watching the lights and street numbers carelessly as the taxi zigzagged over to Fifth Avenue and turned into the rather gloomy passage at 86th Street, which affords quick transit through the huge park to the west side of Manhattan. Once or twice he glanced back and, half way through the cutting, he stopped the taxi close to the narrow sidewalk which skirted the stone wall.

"There is a taxi following me," he told the driver. "Just wait a minute till we see what happens. And you had better take this five dollar bill in case I leave you suddenly."

The driver took the five dollar bill. His face was expressionless, but he felt for the length of lead pipe which lay at his feet. He, too, knew his New York, where anything may happen. It was just as well to be prepared, and a lead pipe is good preparation.

The following cab hesitated and stopped some twenty feet in the rear, the driver turning his head to talk with a single passenger who seemed to be a young man. Wentworth stepped out upon the narrow sidewalk, upon which there were no other pedestrians in sight, and nonchalantly strolled back to the other taxi.

"Interested in me?" he asked, suddenly opening the door of the young man's taxi.

The young man tried to cover his confusion by blowing cigarette smoke through his nose in what he intended to be an extremely worldly-wise manner.

"Newspaper reporter, eh?" remarked Wentworth interrogatively.

"Holy smoke!" gasped the young man. "How did you know that?"

"What else could you be? You're not a crook and you're not a policeman. I can tell that by looking at you."

A third car drew up about twenty feet behind the second one. In it were several men, although their faces could not be distinguished by the poor lighting of the narrow road between the stone walls. Few cars were passing and nobody was using the sidewalk.

Wentworth glanced at the third car and realized that it probably held great danger for him. It was not his nature to run away from danger, but he had serious work ahead of him which could not be delayed.

"There is no use trying to fool you. Mr. Wentworth," said the reporter rather humbly. "I'm Sparks of *The Evening Standard* and I'm assigned to get a story from you about the murders at your apartment."

"Story, eh?" Wentworth shot another quick glance at the third taxi. "Well, I think I shall give you one."

"Will it be exclusive, Mr. Wentworth?" asked the reporter eagerly.

"Absolutely!" Wentworth assured him. "Got a notebook? Good! Get ready to write."

As he spoke, Wentworth placed a foot on the running board and his hands upon the top of the taxi. With the agility of a wild animal he vaulted to the taxi's roof, crouched for a second and sprang easily, slender cane in one hand, and opera hat firm upon his head, to the top of the stone wall. Three shots rang out from the third taxi in rapid succession, even as he leaped into the shelter of the trees and bushes of Central Park.

A LITTLE later Richard Wentworth, striding rapidly, emerged from Central Park somewhat farther uptown and turned his course westward. It was not a fashionable part of town. Evening clothes were mostly worn by waiters, and opera hats were curiosities seldom seen. Children stopped and stared, passing remarks. Women nudged their escorts and pretended that they disapproved. Through it all Wentworth walked swiftly and unconcernedly, yet with eyes that watched, until he came to a house between Amsterdam Avenue and Broadway. So far as he could discern, he was not followed.

It was a brownstone house into which Wentworth finally

turned, ascending the high steps quite as if it were his home. Inside the front door he found a small hall containing dilapidated letter boxes, indicating that the old residence had been converted to a rooming house. One of the letter boxes bore the name of Dorothy Canfield and showed that she lived on the top floor at the back.

The inner vestibule door was locked, but Wentworth did not press the button above her letter box to announce his arrival. Instead, he took out a bunch of slender keys, selected one and turned it deftly in the lock. The door opened.

Inside the door a weak electric light revealed the usual narrow stairs with a worn carpet. A very dim light burned upstairs at the first landing. Everything indicated the drab, economical life which must be lived by people who reside in such a place. Nowhere was evident any sign of vice or crime.

Quietly and quite unseen Wentworth ascended the narrow stairs to the first landing. Doors were closed and showed no lights from within. He ascended the next flight of stairs and came to the bottom of the third flight which was still narrower and bare of carpet. Beside him no lights showed beneath the doors and all was quiet. The landing above him seemed to be in darkness.

Slowly he ascended, but with some slight sound because of the bare steps, and stood upon the top landing. There was just enough light to make two doors distinguishable. The rear door, which should be that of Dorothy Canfield, showed no light. But a faint streak of light could be seen beneath the other door.

Wishing to reconnoiter his surroundings, Wentworth stepped

softly to the door of the lighted room and listened. Regular, deep breathing could be heard. Very gently he turned the knob and found the door unlocked. He pushed it open a bit and looked into the room. On a bed lay a man with his face to the wall, snoring regularly. His left arm hung drunkenly over his side allowing his hand to dangle behind his back. On a table was a whisky bottle and a glass partly filled. The scene seemed to tell a story of poverty and the attempt to drown sorrow in strong drink.

And yet, just as Wentworth was closing the door, his eye noticed the dangling hand. Upon the little finger was a very large ring, marquise in shape and apparently antique. He hesitated. The ring was unquestionably a valuable one, and the incongruity of its presence on the finger of such a man seemed to amuse Wentworth. He was smiling as he backed silently out of the room, and closed the door behind him with no tell-tale sound from the clicking latch.

DOROTHY CANFIELD'S door was also unlocked, and only faint light from a single window entered the room. With the hand which opened the door, Wentworth felt behind it with the light cane which he carried. There was nobody standing there. He stepped quickly into the room and stood with his back to the wall close to the open door, while his eyes became accustomed to the faint light.

The room was sparsely furnished. A small bed loomed against the wall, and a cheap chest of drawers with a small mirror stood by the single window. One electric light bulb hung from the center of the ceiling and on the floor, beneath it, a chair seemed to be overturned. There was complete silence.

Finding no wall switch Wentworth stepped out into the room and turned on the electric light bulb. The light revealed very little more to him than he had seen in the semi-darkness. There was one exception. A closet door stood at the foot of the bed, something he had failed to notice because he had been standing with his back to the wall which contained the door. On examination he found the closet to be locked, with the key on the outside.

Deciding to examine the room minutely before exploring the closet, Wentworth closed the bedroom door and locked it on the inside. The lock was frail, but it would be sufficient to guard him against surprise.

The bed seemed clean and was neatly made. On the bureau were some simple toilet articles and, although inexpensive, they were in good taste. He pulled open some of the bureau drawers and coolly examined some of the intimate things which a woman wears. All were inexpensive. Some handkerchiefs were marked with the letter D, and Wentworth thought of the name of the girl who had sent for him, Dorothy Canfield.

Then the searcher received a surprise. Just as he was closing a top drawer, he noticed a newspaper clipping. It was a cutting from a rotogravure section and he found himself looking at a picture of *himself*. It was from a photograph which had been taken of him in polo costume just after a game which he had played on Long Island two years back. He whistled softly, then spun sharply on his feet as he thought he heard a sound.

Crossing to the bedroom door he unlocked it quietly and flung it swiftly open with his left hand, his cane raised as if to lunge. But there appeared to be nobody in the hall. Frowning, he closed the door and locked it again.

Then it was that he received another surprise. A wire ran along the footboard of the wall against which the bed stood. He looked quickly under the bed, where the wire led, and discovered a telephone. It stood upon the floor where the occupant of the bed could easily reach down beside the wall and lift the receiver to her ear. But why a telephone? How could the occupant of such a room afford to have one?

Wentworth took off his hat and placed it upon the bureau out of respect to his theatrical friends who held the superstition that a hat upon a bed was bad luck. He cared nothing for superstitions himself, but he accustomed himself to humoring his friends. His face showed pleasure. The case was presenting interesting signs. Finally be leaned across the bed, picked up the telephone and called, his own apartment.

Shortly he was speaking to his friend the inspector who was in charge for the night.

"I am at the Canfield girl's room," Wentworth said, speaking in a voice so low that nobody listening at the door could distinguish his words, if they heard at all. "She seems to have departed for parts unknown. It's nine o'clock now. If you don't hear from me again before ten, put some good men on her trail and dig her up."

"Right!" agreed the inspector. "What about yourself, Mr. Wentworth?"

"I expect that the man I want will strike at me here," explained Wentworth. "At any rate I intend to wait here for him, or anybody else who may be interested in me, until ten o'clock. Don't bother about me. Get a little sleep. Remember that the boat with the Spider docks tomorrow and you will need to be fresh if you catch that gentleman."

"As if we didn't have enough trouble without the Spider coming to town!" grumbled the inspector as the telephone conversation ended.

As Wentworth, leaning over the bed, replaced the telephone upon the floor, he suddenly became tense. The strange sound had occurred again. This time there could be no doubt. It seemed like a shuffling or kicking, and it appeared to be coming from the locked closet!

WENTWORTH SLIPPED soundlessly from the bed to his feet and approached the closet door, cane in hand. His eyes showed his keen interest and even his pleasure. The case was becoming more and more puzzling. Little things, but strange things, were adding themselves to it. Big things and direful things might be upon him at any moment. Such situations were to him as wine to other men. Again the sound occurred. Something alive was behind the locked door.

Gently he unlocked the door and swung it outward, standing to one side with cane raised as if to poke inquisitively or to lunge as the occasion might require. He did neither.

Some clothes were hanging in the closet, and below them was exposed the lower half of a silk-clad leg. The ankle was exquisite, and the contour of the calf was perfect.

The leg kicked a little, and Wentworth swept the hanging clothes to one side with his cane. On the floor of the closet a woman lay crumpled. Her hands were tied behind her by means of a stocking, and a man's large handkerchief was an effective gag which stopped her speech. She was a young woman, magnificently and femininely formed as was plainly shown by the clinging and expensive evening gown which she wore. Her face was marred by the gag, but her eyes blazed fury under a great mass of golden hair.

If this was a trap, Wentworth could not believe it. He tossed his cane upon the bed and picked the woman from the closet floor, carrying her to the bed as easily as if she had been a child. Seating her upon the bed, he deftly removed her bindings and stood off in the center of the room to observe what he had found. Her face, with the gag removed, was a trifle hard even as her fury died away. Yet it was a face that would be considered very attractive by most men.

She did not speak at first, nor did Wentworth. Rapidly she opened a handbag which hung upon her arm and took out a vanity mirror, shooting quick glances at the man before her as she began to doctor her complexion.

While she worked upon her face, Wentworth picked up his cane and used it to fish a small shoe out of the closet. He carelessly poked the shoe across the floor until it lay beside the woman's foot, where it was quite apparent that it was much too small to be worn by her.

"Evidently you are not Miss Dorothy Canfield," remarked Wentworth indifferently.

She did not look at him for a moment, and then turned her face to his.

"No," she returned quite calmly. "I got into this room by mistake. Some man jumped on me from behind and tied me up before I knew what was happening. I was looking for a sick friend in the profession."

"Oh! Then you are theatrical?"

She nodded and spoke languidly while she worked at her lips. "Uh-huh, Radio. Resting just now."

Wentworth knew that "resting" probably meant that she was out of a job or that she had taken up something easier and more lucrative.

"Radio accounts for my not having seen you," he remarked. "Certainly I could never have forgotten so beautiful a face—and figure."

She looked pleased at the compliment. "I am Madame Pompé," she said. "I put on the 'pom-pom' radio songs."

"Ah, yes," replied Wentworth, dimly remembering the silly pom-pom songs which had crazed Broadway a few years earlier. "Permit me to give you my card."

He sat on the bed beside her and took out his pocketbook. As he extracted a card he exposed a rather large roll of bills of high denominations. For a moment she stopped working upon her face as her eyes glimpsed so much money, something he noted as he handed her his card.

"Mr. Richard Wentworth," she read, and she was either a superb actress or she really did not know him. Her eyes became dreamy as she regarded him over the card she held in her hand. "You know, Mr. Wentworth, you are frightfully strong."

"Strong?"

"The easy way you carried me to the—over here."

He laughed pleasantly, and as if he were a little embarrassed. "I thought you were too angry to know what was happening to you," he replied, "when I carried you to the—over here." It seemed as though it was going to be easier than he had expected.

He turned toward her, his back to the bedroom door, and looked into her eyes. Behind him the key began to turn noiselessly in the lock, caught by delicate pliers from the outside! SHE WAS smiling her prettiest when the door behind him slowly opened and a masked man stood on the threshold. Then her eyes caught the standing figure vaguely, and fear sprang into them as she looked up.

It was the fear in her eyes which warned Wentworth and caused him to dart one hopeless glance at his opera hat upon the bureau across the room. The distance was too great for him to cover if his danger was imminent. With the cane in his hand he sprang to his feet and whirled, animal-like, to face the door.

The masked man threw out his hand, and a silken cord shot over Wentworth's head and circled his neck.

Wentworth saw the flying loop but could only draw in his chin in an endeavor to protect the front of his throat. There was a strong jerk upon the cord as the noose went snug. He fell to his knees, lunging out with the light cane in his hand as everything began to go black before his eyes.

The cane seemed a futile thing in such an encounter. The sinister strangler, fully as tall and powerful a man as Wentworth, seized the cane roughly in his free hand.

Wentworth, upon his knees and seeing very little, pulled back weakly upon the cane. He pulled weakly, but out from the wooden sheathing slid a slender, gleaming rapier. Again he lunged, desperately, almost blindly. The sharp pointed rapier met the thigh of his antagonist and pierced it, just missing the bone.

There was a cry of rage and pain as the masked man sprang backward into the hall, cursing.

Almost choking for breath, Wentworth managed to kick the door closed and, rapier in hand, lay upon the floor with his feet against it while he tore at the silken cord still circling his neck.

The cord came free, and he struggled into a sitting position with his feet still against the door. Over his shoulder he looked for the woman. The room was empty. Madame Pompé, if that were really her name, must have fled into the hall while his eyes were half blinded by the choking.

He rose to his feet, stretched himself and smiled grimly. He secured his hat, reassembled his rapier stick and opened the bedroom door. The upper hall was empty and, as he expected, the front bedroom was also empty. The drunken man, with the big ring upon the little finger of his left hand, had vanished, leaving behind him the whisky bottle and the partly filled glass.

Wentworth was about to depart when his eye caught a small slip of paper which lay upon the floor almost under his foot.

He picked it up and found a few words scrawled upon it in pencil. They read: "Molly Ann, 96th St., Pier."

CHAPTER 8
THE MOLLY ANN

QUESTIONS FLOODED rapidly through Wentworth's mind. Had the slip of paper been dropped by the man who had attacked him, the man he was hunting? Did the 96th Street pier refer to the East River or the Hudson River? Was Molly Ann a woman or a ship? Although he might be wasting very valuable time, Wentworth decided that he would make some investigation.

Evening clothes and opera hats are not the usual attire in which to investigate New York water fronts. But Richard Wentworth was accustomed to doing things in ways that were different, and his audacity usually won him success. So it was that he bought a new collar to replace the one which had been ruined by the strangler's cord and took the Westside subway to 96th Street.

Leaving the subway station on Broadway, Wentworth sauntered the two blocks which brought him to the entrance of several dilapidated piers jutting out into the Hudson River.

The piers were unlighted and, in the dark, seemed to be quite deserted. Crossing the tracks of the New York Central Railroad, where a dim light shone through a watchman's dingy window, Wentworth accustomed his eyes to the gloom and finally discerned that the pier immediately in front of him was occupied

The sharp pointed rapier met
the thigh of the antagonist....

by some coal barges waiting to deliver their cargo when work commenced in the morning. To his right two piers were unoccupied. To his left, at the most dilapidated pier, there loomed a small tramp steamer which showed no light at all and appeared to be quite deserted. That steamer, he decided might bear the name of *Molly Ann*. Wentworth did not know, but he advanced to find out.

Riverside Drive, with its miles of shady walks among trees and shrubs, is cut off from the Hudson River by the tracks of the New York Central Railroad. Between the tracks and the river the ground is used for dumping by the city and is a desolate waste of rocks and refuse. Here and there, at the water's edge, homeless men have squatted and built themselves little shacks. There are miles of this sordid territory, relieved only here and there by docks as at 96th Street.

Wentworth did not immediately walk out upon a pier but turned downstream and picked his way in the dark over the rough ground until he came to the steep, rocky bank of the Hudson River. Fifty yards upstream could be seen the black outline of the tramp steamer where it was made fast to the rotting pier. Not a vestige of light shone from it. He could discern no stir of movement, no slightest sound of any activity.

Slowly and quietly Wentworth picked his way among the big boulders toward the pier with the black and silent steamer. But had taken only a few steps when he halted and drew back. A light had suddenly shone in his face. It came from an oil lamp in the window of one of the little squatter shacks which nestled between two huge boulders, seeking shelter from the wind. If Wentworth had taken a few more steps he might have stepped off the next boulder upon the roof of the flimsy little structure.

As he hesitated, the door of the shack opened and a man emerged. There was just enough light to make it plain that the man was carrying another man, apparently dead.

Wentworth stepped swiftly forward into the light from the window of the shack. The man dropped his burden and sprang away, trying to escape toward the railroad tracks. But Wentworth, moving with incredible speed, caught him by an arm and jerked him back. He was a large man and a rough man, but poor food and squalid existence had left him no match for Wentworth, who pulled him into the little shack and threw him down upon a filthy mattress which was spread over one half of the floor.

Confident that the man was cowed, Wentworth stood in the doorway and played his flashlight upon the body which the man had dropped in his fright. It was a gruesome sight. There was a face ghastly in death, the face of one of those undernourished creatures who have wandered the earth without work longer than the spirit can survive. There were two articles of clothing, both soggy with water and blood, an undershirt and a pair of pants. So frail was the clothing that it did not conceal what had been done. The man had practically been disemboweled.

Wentworth turned back into the shack and looked at the wreck of a man still lying upon the mattress which was the only thing with which the shack was furnished except for a box upon which stood an oil lamp.

"I didn't do it, mister!" whined the terrified man. "I didn't do it!"

"No," replied Wentworth, "I don't think you have enough guts to do such a thing." He tossed the man a cigarette and watched him while he tremblingly lit it from the heat at the top of the lamp chimney. "You might tell me about it."

Half crying and nervously shaking from physical exhaustion, the man told his story haltingly. He was beginning to be soothed a little by the calm man who stood by the door, the only exit, lazily smoking while he listened.

IT WAS Joe who told the story. That was the name he gave himself. The dead man was just Bill. Joe and Bill had been pals for the last few months of their miserable and sordid lives. This evening after dark they had climbed on board the old tramp steamer, looking for firewood, a piece of old tarpaulin, a broken chair or anything to add to their comfort. No doubt it was stealing, but it was not stealing of a vicious nature.

The old tramp steamer had appeared dark and deserted ever since they had built their tiny shack between the two big boulders on the bank of the Hudson. Neither Joe nor Bill had the slightest suspicion that anybody was aboard the old hulk. They had climbed up a mooring line and dropped down into the forward well beneath the bridge. At least Bill had dropped off the gunwale to the deck. Joe had hesitated, which probably saved his life.

For Bill's feet had scarcely touched the deck when a huge and ferocious man—so Joe described him—darted down the companionway from the deckhouse and rushed at Bill. Bill tried to run away, but the big man shot out an arm on the end of which was a great, sharp hook. Joe said it was like an immense fish hook only that it had no barb.

"A one-armed man or at least a man who had lost one of his hands," commented Wentworth, tossing another cigarette to the man on the mattress.

Joe nodded. He told how the ugly hook had entered Bill's stomach, through the thin undershirt, and how it had cruelly been jerked so that it tore downward through the wretched man's bowels. He told how the murderer had lifted the bleeding, dying man and tossed him over the bulwark into the water.

Bill's body had scarcely splashed into the water before Joe had slid back to the pier on the mooring line and had dropped quietly into the water to try to rescue his pal. He had found the inert body and towed it ashore and carried it into the little shack. But Bill was quite dead and Joe, afraid that he would be blamed by the police, was about to throw the body back into the Hudson when Wentworth had discovered him.

"Do you think that the man with the hook saw you, Joe?" asked Wentworth.

"No, mister, he didn't see me at all."

"And do you know the name of that tramp steamer, Joe?"

"Sure, mister! It's the *Molly Ann*."

Wentworth took out his cigarette case and placed half of his cigarettes on the box beside the lamp. On top of the cigarettes he placed a twenty-dollar bill. Then he passed out of the wretched shack and out of Joe's life, stepping carefully around the horrid sight which lay, bloody, by the door.

He had found the name of the old tramp steamer at the scene of the attack upon himself. Even before he reached it, murder had been committed upon it. There seemed little doubt in his mind that this old ship was in some way connected with the criminal he was trying to destroy. Slowly and carefully he made his way along the boulder-strewn riverbank until he came to the entrance of the old and rotting pier to which was moored the lightless and apparently lifeless ship.

HE WALKED slowly and silently down the middle of the pier. As he passed the old ship with its patches of red lead just visible in the starlight, he thought that he saw a head above the bulwark of the forward well, but he could not be sure. He knew that he was far more visible to anybody on the ship than such a person would be visible from the pier.

The ship had its stern out into the stream and he passed on until he came opposite the aft well. Here again he thought that he caught a glimpse of a man peering at him over the bulwark. He paused, and after a few moments he was certain of it.

Since he was being watched, Wentworth decided that nothing was to be gained by any kind of concealment. He seated himself upon the pier and lit a cigarette while he considered the situation. The ship was attached to the dock by a bow line and a stern line and, there being no gangplank down, there was no way of reaching the deck except by climbing one of those lines. It would be impossible, he decided, to gain the deck in such a way against a murderous man who wished to bar the way.

What, then, was to be done? It was easy enough for Wentworth to think of a number of schemes of attack upon the vessel.

But these schemes involved launches and lines, or rope ladders with hooks, and the assistance of others, or at least with the assistance of the faithful Ram Singh. Such preparations required time and Wentworth had other things to do. Yet he refused to depart without making some kind of investigation or striking some blow.

The brutal murder had infuriated him, and he wanted nothing better than to meet the one-armed man with the iron hook.

He decided, finally, that it might be possible to make somebody, the man with the hook preferably, come off the ship. The ship was on the upstream side of the dock and the tide, going out, was pressing it against the dock. In consequence the mooring lines were loose.

Wentworth walked across to the aft mooring line and lifted the heavy hawser from its mooring pin, dropping it upon the dock. Then he went back to the opposite side of the pier and sat down to finish his cigarette. Had his act been seen? When the tide turned the stern of the ship would drift away from the dock, if someone did not descend and replace the hawser. He hoped that he would not have to wait so long, and he did not hope in vain.

A dark figure mounted upon the forward bulwark, reached for the mooring line and slid down it to the dock like an arrow. Certainly the man was athletic, and he seemed to be unusually large. Reaching the dock at the bow of the ship, he had cut Wentworth off from the land. If the man proved to be in a fighting mood there would be no way to escape him except by jumping into the water. Wentworth sat smoking and watching.

Down the center of the pier came the figure of the big man. He came fast and he came straight toward Wentworth who rose and tossed his cigarette into the water. The oncoming man paused at a distance of about ten feet and stared at Wentworth, puzzled at the sight of a man in evening clothes upon such a lonely dock at such a time.

"What the hell did you cast that line off for?" he demanded.

It was then that Wentworth saw the long and devilish, iron hook protruding from the partly empty sleeve of the man's right arm.

"I thought that I should like to meet the fellow who rips out men's guts," returned Wentworth quietly.

THE MAN stopped, staring, then flung up his maimed arm with the hook and sprang at Wentworth. But he sprang at nothing, for when he landed, Wentworth was not there.

A sharp pain in his left arm warned him that something had happened to him. Surprised, he saw that Wentworth had sprung backward with the agility of a fencer and was standing, right foot forward, with a slender, gleaming blade in his hand. Astonished, he felt his left arm by pressing it against his face, having no right hand, and realized that it was this blade which had pricked him.

More cautiously now the man advanced again upon Wentworth, sweeping the air before him with the great hook to ward off the snake-like, circling blade. But the blade darted here and there and could not be stopped. It pierced his thigh, drew blood from his cheek, nicked his chest.

The one-armed man hesitated and drew back a little. Toughened by many a seaport brawl, he was not to be beaten by pin pricks administered by a toylike, glittering blade. Never before had he encountered a man in evening clothes who fought with a rapier. A cutlass would have been more to his understanding, but even cutlasses had almost vanished from seafaring life.

He advanced still more cautiously with the long, iron hook extended at the end of his reach. If he could catch that dancing blade in his hook he could snap it or wrench the weapon from his antagonist. There was not fear in his heart, only rage and the wish to kill.

Wentworth knew the danger of permitting his blade to be caught by the hook. The light was poor for both fighters. But the man with the hook had his back to the rising ground, which almost shrouded him; while Wentworth had his back to the water, which caught some of the starlight and exposed him to his antagonist. Slowly he gave way, backing toward the end of the pier, watching for an opportunity to lunge. It was vitally necessary for him to find that opportunity before he reached the spot from which, with only water behind him, he could retreat no farther.

In the faint starlight the duel continued. Blood dripped from the one-armed man, but he had fought many a bloodier battle and he pressed on cautiously. At last Wentworth had his back close to the water. One more step in retreat would take him into the river. He had to end the fight at once or lose the battle.

At the last moment as the fencer stood upon the very end of the pier, there was the clash of metal upon metal. The rapier was caught in the iron hook! Infuriated and cursing, the one-armed man, wrenched back to disarm his antagonist. It seemed as though the slender rapier had been rendered useless.

But Wentworth's mind worked with the speed of his own blade. He could not dislodge his weapon and he could not resist the backward pull of the heavy man he was fighting. Therefore he pressed *forward*—lunged! The blade, unable to retire, found it easy to advance, sliding through the iron hook until it had entered the chest and protruded from the back of the man who had so brutally murdered the humble squatter called Bill!

The greater ruffian, with his ugly hook, sank backward and lay upon the old, rotting dock with sightless eyes directed toward the stars which they could not see. Very methodically Wentworth wiped the blade upon the man's coat and returned it to its walking-stick sheath. He knelt beside the ugly, lifeless face and pressed the little Spider seal upon the coarse forehead.

Rapidly Wentworth climbed the forward mooring line and sat upon the bulwark, looking down into the forward well of the *Molly Ann*. In the dim light he could see great, metal cylinders ranged side by side. They were unusual objects to be seen upon such a tramp steamer, and he was about to climb down for a closer inspection when a beam of light flashed over the steamer and warned him of a new danger for a man who sometimes took the law into his own hands.

The beam of light came from the river. It left the old tramp steamer and played upon the rotting pier. Nosing up to the dock, upon inquisitive inspection, was a police boat. There was just time for Wentworth to slide down the mooring line and to retreat into the shadows at the pier entrance, before a shout came from one of the river police upon the boat. Their light had played upon the dead man.

It was only a matter of a few minutes before the police would know that the man was neither asleep nor drunk. In a very short time word would be flashed to Police Headquarters that the Spider had made another killing.

Reluctantly Wentworth gave up all idea of further investigation of the *Molly Ann* that night.

CHAPTER 9
INTO THE NIGHT

AT THE Park Avenue apartment of Richard Wentworth much energy and thought was being expended. Outlying buildings, which gave a view upon the bullet-pierced window of the music room, were more and more closely studied, and large diagrams were drawn by the experts who specialized in the science of the motion of projectiles. It was pretty definitely established that the bullet must have come from the upper portion of a large apartment house on the next avenue, and that it had been fired from a high-powered sporting rifle, probably with telescopic sights. The experts, however, could not be certain from which window the bullet had been fired, and detectives were checking up on all the inmates of the apartment building.

The inspector in charge of the case was worried. They had made scant progress toward running down the would-be murderer, and the Police Department would be treated very roughly by the morning newspapers, if no arrests could be reported. To add to his discomfit he was puzzled by a report that a shooting had occurred in Central Park. And he was mystified by a rumor that the shooting had been in connection with an attack upon Richard Wentworth.

At ten o'clock, not having heard again from Wentworth, he sent detectives to the rooming house of Dorothy Canfield, with orders to trace that young woman and to bring her in for questioning. Almost continuously he sat with a telephone at his ear, receiving reports and giving sharp orders and brief suggestions.

At half past ten the butler admitted a young woman, really only a girl, very small and exceedingly pretty.

"I want to see Mr. Richard Wentworth," she said.

"Mr. Wentworth is not at home, Miss," answered the butler.

The girl gave a little cry of alarm as a policeman came into the entrance hall. She turned and tried to escape through the door, but was easily stopped by the officer.

A plainclothesman entered swiftly and took the girl by the arm, leading her to one side, shooting sharp questions. The girl jerked away from him, opened her handbag and took out a small bottle which she raised to her lips, trying to extract the cork with her teeth. The detective grabbed the bottle out of her hand, glanced at it and called the inspector.

"Here is a young girl trying to commit suicide," he said, handing the bottle to the inspector.

"Are you Dorothy Canfield?" the inspector asked after a glance at the bottle and a quick scrutiny of the new arrival.

The girl nodded nervously, and the inspector led her into the music room, while the amazed butler shrugged his shoulders in dismay and returned to the butler's pantry for a cigarette and a glass of sherry.

HE SELECTED a biscuit and placed his hand upon the decanter of sherry, just as the bell sounded again, the annunciator this time indicating the service door. Very cautiously he opened the door as two men evidently of the servant type came out of the service elevator carrying large hampers.

The men stated that they were temporary waiters, bringing hampers containing a cold supper which Mr. Wentworth desired to have served at midnight. One of the waiters, rather old and stooped, with graying hair, started to carry his hamper inside when he was stopped by a detective who came swiftly through the kitchen.

"What's the big idea?" the waiter exclaimed, placing his hamper upon the floor and noticing a uniformed man behind the detective. "Is this place pinched? What kind of a place is it?"

"This place is all right," remarked the detective. "Let's see what you have in those baskets."

"I don't like the police," grumbled the old waiter and darted back into the elevator. "I'm going to get out of here."

The detective strode into the elevator and roughly pulled the old man out. Without wasting any further words, he dragged him through the kitchen and into the music room, where the inspector and several detectives were subjecting Dorothy Canfield to a continuous fire of questions.

"Here's a guy, inspector," the detective announced, "who

doesn't like cops and who tried to run away. Says he's a waiter from a caterer sent by Mr. Wentworth. I think he's lying."

The old waiter fidgeted nervously beside his captor. His bowed head and stooped body seemed none too well supported by weak legs. He stared with apparent fear at the pathetic spectacle of the diminutive Dorothy Canfield, forced to face a powerful light while she met the shrewd gaze of her police inquisitors and listened to the reiteration of their searching questions.

"I shall be with you in a minute," the inspector said to the detective and turned back to the girl. "Now, Miss Canfield, we'll keep you here till you tell us the truth. You might as well come through with it."

"I ain't stoppin' here any longer," whined the old waiter.

"Shut up!" growled the detective.

The growl seemed to unnerve the decrepit waiter so that he swayed against the detective and nearly slipped to the floor.

"Stand up!" the detective growled more loudly, jerking his captive roughly into a standing position.

With surprising agility the waiter slipped from the detective's grasp and hobbled rapidly across the room to the group surrounding the wretched girl. The inspector rose angrily to meet him.

"Take this," whined the waiter, thrusting a pistol abruptly into the inspector's hand.

"Why, it's a police pistol!" exclaimed the inspector, examining the weapon. "Where the devil did you get it, my man?"

"Holy smoke!" ejaculated the detective. The son of a gun took my pistol away from me!"

In the strong light which was playing upon the girl the figure of the waiter grew taller as he slowly straightened up. Even in his ill-fitting waiter's clothes his well-knit, lithe form became apparent. The expression of his face changed, became strong and alert.

"Mr. Wentworth!" exclaimed the inspector, gazing at the transformed man in the strong light.

"Exactly," Wentworth returned, taking the pistol out of the inspector's hand and returning it to the astounded detective. "Thought I would do a little impersonating myself."

"But why?" demanded the inspector. "Why did you wish to impersonate a waiter?"

"Two reasons," answered Wentworth. "I wished to bring in a new cook, and some food, and know that neither had been tampered with; also I wish to mystify my enemy by returning to my apartment without his knowledge."

Deliberately Wentworth switched off the powerful light which had been shining in Dorothy Canfield's eyes.

HE SMILED at the inspector. "I had an appointment with this young lady," he said, "but, for some reason, she did not wait for me." Ram Singh came to the door of the music room and departed upon receiving a few words in his native language from his master. "I was attacked by the man we are hunting and succeeded in wounding him, how badly I do not know. He got away. That is all I have to report at present, inspector."

"This Canfield woman can tell us something," the inspector insisted. "We'll break her down very soon now."

"I think not," remarked Wentworth drily. "In the first place, Miss Dorothy Canfield is my guest and, in the second place, my dear inspector, you don't know very much about women."

"She tried to take poison," the inspector persisted, "and we just stopped her in time. She *must* know something."

"Of course she knows something. I congratulate you upon saving her life. But, still, my dear inspector, I maintain that you don't know much about women."

Ram Singh came into the room with a dressing gown of green silk which he threw over his master's shoulders completely hiding the somewhat dilapidated waiter's clothes. The subtle makeup around his eyes and his grayed hair robbed him of some of his natural attraction, but left him with an air of mystery. There was nothing left of the weak character which he had portrayed so cleverly upon entering the room.

The inspector was somewhat nettled, yet he could not help admiring the unusual man who stood before him. "What do you intend to do?" he asked.

"Men who make up their minds in advance," was the slow, enigmatical reply, "are almost always at a disadvantage when the time for action comes. Perhaps you will be kind enough to leave me."

The inspector shrugged and walked out of the room followed by the detective. At a sign from his master, Ram Singh also withdrew and closed the door of the music room.

ALONE WITH the nervous and almost terror stricken girl,

the man in the soft, green dressing gown did not approach her or even speak to her. Instead, he walked away from her and seated himself upon the organ bench at the end of the room.

For a little while there was silence and nothing seemed to happen. The girl in the chair turned her head tensely to watch the green-clad man who sat upon the organ bench with his back to her. She was quite unaware of the small mirror which permitted him to view her as he sat there. So gradually that she scarcely noticed it at first the indirect lighting of the room commenced to dim as his hand slowly turned a rheostat conveniently placed below the keyboard of the organ. She relaxed somewhat with the softening of the light and allowed her head to rest against the back of the chair.

When the light was quite soft, the music commenced. In the beginning it was so low and gentle that it was scarcely audible. There was sorrow in it and hope, and it held strength even when it could scarcely be heard. It was an improvisation by a man who allowed himself to imagine the feelings of a woman. Sometimes the music was religious and a little Eastern and sometimes there was a hint of the martial which was always dispelled by romance.

Her eyes closed and her fingers ceased to grip the arms of her chair.

The music lowered to a soft trembling and ended as he turned on the bench and faced her.

"I should like to help you."

She did not open her eyes. She was really very young, almost like a tired child who clings to sleep and does not want to commence the day again.

He continued softly: "You have a sweetheart"—she opened her eyes and stared at him incredulously—"who is wanted by the police."

"He didn't do it!" she exclaimed vehemently. "He didn't do it!"

"I know that he didn't do it!"

"I know that he didn't," very softly.

"Then—then why—"

There were tears in her eyes, tears that came with the birth of hope.

"My dear," he continued as if talking to a tired child, but with nothing belittling in his voice, "I have been working on your case for months and it is now time that I found your sweetheart. I believe that he telephones you from various pay stations at night, but is afraid to come near you, fearing the police."

She nodded. "And then a strange man telephoned to me and tried to make me tell him Jack Selwyn's address. He said that it would be all right if I told him but that, if I didn't tell him, he would tell the police that I knew where Jack was living and that the police would soon get the address out of me. I got desperate and decided to end it all rather than let Jack go to prison. I was just going to do it when—I thought of you."

"But what made you think of me, Dorothy?" he asked, so gently that she did not notice he had used her first name.

"Two or three times the newspapers told about some very

clever things you did when you worked with the police and how you showed them up to be all wrong. They were hunting my Jack, and I wanted you to show them that they were wrong again."

"That seems rather strange as my name was not mentioned very prominently," he said, turning back to the organ and playing softly for a few moments.

"But—" she commenced and stopped.

"Yes?" he inquired without turning to look at her.

"But I knew you so well," she continued, "because I used to see pictures of you in the newspapers when you played polo and—and, well I suppose I would have fallen in love with you if I hadn't met Jack."

"I hope Jack is a fine chap," he replied, turning toward her with a smile. "Going to trust me?"

She looked at him gravely with very large eyes. "I think," she said slowly, "that any woman would trust you."

Still smiling, he handed her a waiter's pad and pencil which he took from the shabby coat underneath his dressing gown. "Just write Jack's address for me in case these bothersome policemen have planted a dictaphone in my music room," he said quietly.

SHE SCRIBBLED upon the pad, and he gave it a single glance before tearing off the top page and touching a match to it. "Now nobody can know except you and me," he said when the flame had done its work. "By the way, was it Jack who tied up the strange woman in your room and locked her in the closet?"

"Yes," she replied. "I was talking with Jack on the telephone when she came into the room and I put the telephone down without hanging up the receiver. I screamed when she twisted my arm because I refused to give her Jack's address. Jack heard me scream over the telephone and came running over to my room."

"I don't suppose," he said, looking at her thoughtfully, "that you know why these people wish to obtain Jack's address?"

"No," she said, shaking her head emphatically, "and neither does Jack."

The door opened and Nita van Sloan entered.

"Dick!" exclaimed Nita. "What on earth are you doing in that costume and what have you done to your face?"

"Nita," said Wentworth, "let me introduce Miss Dorothy Canfield. Dorothy, this is my very good friend, Miss Van Sloan."

"You look a little faint, Dorothy," said Nita, extending her hand with friendliness and instantly noticing the girl's extreme youth. "I think a glass of champagne would be good for you."

Nita, who sensed much more than she had yet learned, took charge of Dorothy in a way that was charming and which placed the girl much at her ease.

As the three of them were passing through the hall on their way to the dining room, Wentworth heard the inspector conversing with one of the detectives.

"I am confident that the bullet was fired from the small penthouse of the apartment building on the next avenue," the inspector remarked.

"From Madame Pompé's penthouse? queried Wentworth, overhearing the remark.

The effect of the query upon the inspector was electrical. "How the devil did you know that Madame Pompé lived in that penthouse?" he almost shouted. "I just received the information over the telephone. How in blazes did you know it?"

"I went through the apartment about an hour ago," cooly stated Wentworth.

"You went through it!" gasped the inspector. "The owner is out and a couple of our best men are trying to get keys that will fit the door."

"They won't find anything inside," replied Wentworth indifferently. "However, if they insist upon getting in, tell 'em to go out on the roof and try the pantry window. It isn't locked. I jimmied it."

While the inspector stared in stupefaction at Wentworth, that very cool individual turned to Nita.

"Can you lend Dorothy some night things?" he asked. "She is spending the night with us."

"Oh, but I can't stay all night!" interrupted Dorothy in alarm. "I am staying with a cousin tonight and she won't know what has happened to me."

"Telephone her or send her a telegram," said Wentworth determinedly. "Your life would not be worth very much if you left this apartment tonight."

Jenkyns came up with an extension telephone and handed it to Wentworth. "Telephone for you, sir."

"My dear Madame Pompé," exclaimed Wentworth with

surprising warmth as soon as he heard the voice. "I've been worried every minute since you disappeared from that room. Fancy that beastly creature barging in on us! He must have been mad. I don't blame you for running away... You are all alone and want me to come over?... Will I come? I most certainly shall—just as soon as I get rid of some bothersome people... Oh, in about an hour. Somebody is coming into the room and I can't talk any more. Till we meet!"

Wentworth grinned at the inspector as he handed the telephone back to the butler. "Now, my dear inspector," he said, "if you will call all your men away from Madame Pompé's apartment building for the remainder of the night, I shall go over there and see what I can do."

As Richard Wentworth finished speaking, his face sobered and his green dressing gown slipped to the floor, revealing him once more in the shabby clothes of a waiter who had seen better days. Slowly his shoulders began to droop and one of his legs bent a little as if with weakness. His lower lip sagged out and his jaw dropped a little, while his eyes closed somewhat and appeared to lose their alertness.

With head bowed he shambled aimlessly from the hall and out through the kitchen entrance, where he pressed the button of the service elevator—on his way once more into the night of New York...

CHAPTER 10
A TRYST WITH DEATH

R ICHARD WENTWORTH walked slowly out of the servants' entrance of the Park Avenue apartment building and turned toward the East-side subway. At the entrance he stooped and picked up a cigarette butt, commenced to place it in his mouth and looked down the subway entrance where smoking is forbidden. Carefully he placed the butt in his pocket and entered the subway… Wentworth was probably as great an artist as the man he was hunting and who was hunting him. One of the two artists would win, and the other would probably meet sudden death.

Considerably down town Wentworth left the subway and entered a small boarding house. He mounted two flights of stairs and knocked upon a door. Sparks of *The Evening Standard* admitted him.

"Gee, Mr. Wentworth!" exclaimed Sparks. "I didn't expect to see you back so soon. Did your trick work?"

"Perfectly," replied Wentworth. "Did you get me a new collar and tie?"

"I did, and I had your dinner coat and trousers pressed."

"Good! Let's get into them. How is your scoop coming on?"

"Front page! It's a pip, Mr. Wentworth, and I sure am grateful to you."

Wentworth changed his clothes rapidly and picked up his opera hat and cane. He snapped the elastic loops in the top of his hat and unconcernedly inserted the small revolver which he took from a pocket of the waiter's clothes.

"Holy smoke!" exclaimed Sparks. "I wondered what those elastic loops were for!"

"Keep the information out of your front-page story and it will be all right with me," commented Wentworth.

"Sure, Mr. Wentworth!" Sparks eyes showed admiration. "I never spill a confidence."

"Is that so?" Wentworth threw himself into a chair and lit a cigarette from a lighter which he regarded contemplatively for a moment before dropping it back into his pocket. "Well, I shall give you something more in confidence, if you will promise me not to use it until I give you permission or—until I am dead."

"It's a bargain!" exclaimed the reporter eagerly.

From a table Wentworth took a sheet of paper, scribbled upon it for a few moments and tossed the sheet to the reporter. "Sparks," he said, "you will notice that I have listed a number of police cases which have occurred during the past two years."

"Uh-huh. I was on most of them and I remember them all."

"Each case involves impersonation or the claim by the accused that impersonation took place."

"Ye-es," agreed the reporter, searching his memory. "By Jove, Mr. Wentworth, that's a fact."

"The same master criminal operated in each case."

The reporter whistled. "But," he argued, "in some of these cases the police obtained convictions and sent the accused to Sing Sing."

"They sent innocent men to Sing Sing." Wentworth puffed at his cigarette. "I tried to convince the police of this, but I was unable to give them sufficient evidence to prove my theory."

"Then it is only a theory?"

"The last of those cases," continued Wentworth, ignoring the interruption, "is the case of Jack Selwyn. You will remember that Selwyn was the confidential clerk of a diamond merchant. He was sent with a package of valuable stones to another diamond merchant. In the hall of the office building, a hall not too well lighted, he claimed that his employer rushed after him and took back the package of diamonds."

"Yes, I remember the case very well," Sparks added. "Later in the day his employer denied that he had taken back the diamonds and telephoned for the police. Selwyn, very much alarmed, rushed out into the street and has never been caught."

"Exactly! Well, the Selwyn case was the last of these impersonation cases in New York. But a case involving the same technique cropped up abroad and I went to Paris in search of this criminal. I nearly caught him, and he nearly caught me—on several occasions. Then he doubled back to New York and actually entered my apartment by impersonating me. He stole a valuable piece of Chinese porcelain and killed a New York detective whom he ran into by chance—a strangulation killing, his favorite method.

"So daring and so clever is this man that he actually does these things without fear of detection by the police. I believe that all these crimes, however, are but steps toward a greater crime which he is now planning—a crime so great that it will, if it is perpetrated, dwarf all his other crimes. He is a great actor, a genius. There is no other man like him."

"Yes, there is," said the reporter slowly while he regarded his companion thoughtfully through his cigarette smoke. "You are a great actor, yourself, Mr. Wentworth. You think like lightning and you act while you think. You could do everything that this criminal has done."

"Strangle my victims, for instance?" queried Wentworth, smiling.

SPARKS, OF *The Evening Standard* looked uncomfortable, but he did not lower his eyes as he continued to regard his companion through the smoke. "Yes, Mr. Wentworth," he said, "I think you could—if you thought the cause justified such an act."

Wentworth laughed, pleasantly and frankly. "You are a good man, Sparks, and—you are right. Your newspaper training has taught you to read character. Are you, by any chance, suggesting that I *am* this criminal?"

"Oh, no!" Sparks was emphatic. "If I thought you *were,* I would be out the door and into the nearest speakeasy to drown my fright before you could tip your opera hat."

"Liar!" The epithet, spoken with good humor, completely won the reporter's heart.

"But I don't understand why you are telling me all this, Mr. Wentworth," said Sparks, pleased by the implied compliment to his courage.

"You witnessed the attack upon me in the park," Wentworth continued, ignoring the remark. "I escaped from it and reached my destination where I met this Pompé woman and frustrated another attack upon my life. I telephoned to you about Madame Pompé. You gave me her address and told me that she had dropped out of radio singing two years ago without any apparent cause.

"Two years ago these impersonating crimes commenced in New York—some brilliant mind went wrong and took to crime. Madame Pompé is connected with the man who owns that brilliant mind." Wentworth's eyes twinkled as he paused. "Have you seen her?"

"Uh-huh. She's an eyeful."

Wentworth chuckled as if he were remembering something. "Such a woman can only have one relation for any man. Madame Pompé is our criminal's 'good time girl,' and that is the reason that I am telling you all this, Sparks."

"Eh? What have I got to do with this seductive radio artist?"

"Not a thing, for your sake, I hope," replied Wentworth, smiling. "But I want you to find out something about her boy friends, or more exactly, about her boy friend, for I do not think our criminal would tolerate any rival."

"I am beginning to get you."

"I believe that a brilliant man, probably a professional man, took to crime and dropped out of society two years ago, at the same time that Madame Pompé dropped out of radio. Today Madame Pompé is connected with the criminal I am hunting. Sparks, I want you to discover for me the name of the man who took this woman away from her radio singing. Think you can do it?"

"Uh-huh, if there is such a man. It's in line with a reporter's work. What a story for the front page—if I ever get a chance to spread it."

"You will get the chance if I live. If I don't live you can do what you like about it."

Richard Wentworth rose from his chair and placed his hat upon his head at the very slight angle which was so effective. He regarded his cane for a moment, then tossed it upon the reporter's bed.

"Rapier stick," he explained. "Excellent steel from Toledo. Used it once tonight, and my enemy might expect me to use it again. Never do what I am expected to do. Run it through the gizzard of anybody who attacks you."

Wentworth picked a telephone from the table and began dialing while Sparks gingerly examined the rapier stick. "Oh, Jenkyns, connect me with Miss Van Sloan."

"It sure is a honey!" muttered Sparks as he drew the slender blade from its sheath. "Holy smoke! It's got *blood* on it." He gazed in awe at the man at the telephone. "What a man!" he breathed reverently.

WENTWORTH SPOKE again over the wire. "Nita? How is your head?"

"It's aching, Dick, but it's getting better."

"I can't tell you how sorry I am, Nita. There are probably a dozen silly detectives listening to our conversation. How is little Dorothy?"

"Asleep. I gave her half a pint of champagne and tucked her into bed."

"Good! And how is the Commissioner?"

"You would be surprised."

"Yes? What has he been doing?"

"Indulging in mild flirtation."

"Oh, come, Nita!" protested Wentworth. "Explain yourself."

"I have been sitting by his bed, holding his hand. He seems to like it."

Wentworth chuckled. "You don't need to work on him, my dear. What about the other policemen? Are they bothering you at all?"

Nita laughed a little. "Not while I am holding the Commissioner's hand. Besides, I have the dining room table all cluttered up with beer, onions and limburger cheese sandwiches. The New York Police Department would go through fire and water for me."

"I might have known it," Wentworth commented. "You can meet any situation that life holds." And then very rapidly in French: "Did Professor Brownlee arrive?"

And in swift, staccato French the reply came: "Yes. With package. I took it. Gave it to Ram Singh."

"Excellent!" Wentworth reverted to English. "You always do the right thing, Nita. Tell Ram Singh I may need him tonight. Now go to bed and get some sleep."

As Wentworth hung up the telephone and turned toward the door, Sparks came toward him, a question on his face.

"Isn't there anything else I can do?" he asked.

"Well," said Wentworth, "you might go down to West 96th Street and have a look at the *Molly Ann*, tied up to a rotting dock. If you notice any activity I would like to know about it. Don't go on board the ship, however, if you value your life."

"I sure will do that little thing," Sparks agreed emphatically. "Where are you going now, Mr. Wentworth?"

"Off to see Madame Pompé. I believe the lady has become the human bait which is supposed to lure me to my death."

Wentworth was smiling when he moved across the room and passed out into the narrow hall.

CHAPTER 11
THE MAN IN THE MASK

A T MADAME POMPÉ'S penthouse Wentworth was admitted by a French maid, Mimi, who was very trim in black and white.

"Monsieur Wentworth? This way please."

He carried his crushed opera hat with him, unnoticed by the maid, and found Madame Pompé lying upon a couch beside a window, from which could be seen the lights of New York City through potted plants which stood, garden-like, around the penthouse upon the roof of the building.

"You will admit nobody else, Mimi," instructed Madame Pompé, turning lazily upon the couch and smiling at Wentworth. "You understand?"

"Mais oui, Madame!" The maid withdrew. Of course she understood. What French maid would not have understood?

"But my servant is coming," Wentworth said.

"Your servant?" she asked in surprise.

"He is bringing a basket of champagne."

"Oh!" She stood up with a pleased smile. Standing, her ivory gown presented the woman both beautifully and very sensationally. She stood perfectly still; it was poise, not pose. "Like it?" she asked candidly and came into movement again.

"Of course," Wentworth answered quietly. "It is far too good for a woman who twists a little girl's arm in a cheap rooming house."

Madame Pompé frowned. "So you discovered that? Well, I had to do it. I couldn't help it. But I didn't have to invite you here tonight. I am playing now. Can't we be friends?"

She seemed so beautiful as she stood before him that it was difficult to believe her dangerous in a criminal way. Wentworth, however, realized that she was a consummate actress.

She fanned herself and he threw open the window beside the couch, letting in a slight breeze from the warm night. Only faint noises ascended from the streets below and drifted into the room through the potted plants which stood upon the roof outside the window.

Then Ram Singh arrived, carrying a basket, majestic under his turban. Mimi was at first frightened at sight of the Oriental, but decided that he was handsome and asked him to come into the pantry for a glass of wine on his way out.

"Not drink!" refused the Oriental contemptuously. "Drink no good!"

Madame Pompé had been even more impressed by Ram Singh than she had been by Wentworth's pocketbook, something Wentworth had been able to detect while he directed the Hindu in the placing of the wine upon a table. The directions, given in Hindustani, had little to do with the wine and much to do with other, more important matters. But Madame Pompé knew no Hindustani and thought only that a man with such a servant must be exceedingly desirable from a worldly point of view.

Wentworth placed his hat carelessly upon a mantelpiece and sat with her beside a small table while they sipped some of the wine from the first of the two bottles which the basket contained.

It was quite evident that Madame Pompé was exercising all her charm, all her physical lure, upon the man who had come to see her.

"Do you know why I invited you to come here tonight?" she asked meaningly.

"Perhaps," Wentworth replied coolly, "you may intend to kill me."

She expressed indignant horror at the thought. And she was clever. She snapped open a small bag which dangled from her wrist and took from it a tiny pistol which she handed to him.

"Would I give you this if I wished to kill you?" she asked quietly.

"You might," he answered casually, accepting the weapon indifferently.

IT WAS a superb piece of workmanship, very small but quite deadly. He examined it with apparent interest, snapping the safety catch off and on. Releasing the little magazine, he dropped it out upon the palm of his hand and ejected the cartridge which lay in the barrel, catching it dexterously and inserting it at the bottom of the magazine.

"You are familiar with pistols," Madame Pompé remarked approvingly.

"Yes," admitted Wentworth. "I have had some little experience with them."

He slid the magazine back into the grip of the pistol and tossed the weapon a full three feet into the air, catching it between his two hands. He opened his hands. The pistol was gone!

"Oh!" she exclaimed in surprise. "That *was* clever. How did you do it?"

"Just on old magician's trick," he explained. "I practice sleight of hand. It amuses me."

"I don't care," she returned. "You can keep the pistol. I gave it to you to show my good faith."

Suddenly Wentworth shot a hand toward her and appeared to pluck the tiny pistol from her bag where it lay open upon her lap.

"And I return it to you," he said.

"To show *your* good faith?" she asked, taking the pistol and tucking it into her bag.

"To show you that I have no fear of you," he answered.

"Oh!"

"And perhaps you had better take the magazine," he added, holding it out on the palm of his hand. "I slipped it out again when you weren't looking."

This time there was a flash of anger in her eyes. She slid the magazine quickly into its place and drew back the bolt to insert the first cartridge in the barrel. Nor did she throw on the safety catch which might delay a shot for the fraction of a second while it was being cast off.

Wentworth smiled a trifle. "Angry?" he asked.

"A woman never likes to be fooled," she returned. "But I wish we could be friends."

"Give me some reasons for it," he suggested.

Swiftly she rose and went to some black portières which hung over the entrance to the hall. She swept them aside. As though satisfied that nobody was eavesdropping, she dropped the portières back into place and returned to her chair.

Their chairs were close together. Slowly she turned sidewise and looked up into his face while she bent forward until her lips were almost touching his. There was slumbering fire in her eyes and a cloying perfume surrounded her head. Her lips parted, invitingly, and she waited.

Wentworth neither advanced his head to the challenge, nor did he withdraw it. He gazed thoughtfully into her upturned face, but he refused the invitation of her lips.

"Come to the point," he said. "What do you want?"

With all the abandon of a woman versed in the wiles of her sex she pleaded with him. She begged him to take her away from a man who was a monster of evil and from whom she could not escape.

Wentworth rose and stood with his back to the mantelpiece, looking down at her.

She rose and stood close before him.

"Take me in your arms again like you did when you found me," she asked, coming still closer to him.

He appeared to be wavering.

Swiftly she slipped her arms around his neck and leaned against him.

"Why do you wait?" she whispered.

It was then that the portières parted and the masked man came into the room, a gun in either hand. His face was completely hidden, but it was obviously the same man who had thrown the silken cord in Dorothy Canfield's room.

He seemed a trifle lame but he came swiftly and so silently that the woman, with her back turned, did not hear.

And Wentworth did not move, although he saw his enemy even as her lips pressed his and he was forced to straighten a little from his leaning position to support her weight.

"Damn!"

With the exclamation the man halted, not five feet from the pair at the mantelpiece, his guns raised menacingly.

And at the sound of that voice Madame Pompé jerked her lips from Wentworth's and turned her head with a cry toward the man with the guns. The next second she turned back to Wentworth and was clinging madly to him, apparently terrified.

If she was acting, it was superb artistry. But Wentworth knew suddenly that it was *not* acting. She was pressed so closely to him that he could feel the wild beating of her heart. In that mad embrace he could only stand quite still. An attempt to reach his opera hat, with the concealed revolver, or to make any other swift move, would only be to invite quick death.

IT WAS Wentworth who spoke first. Cool, careless words

107

came from him, words which seemed to denote utter disregard for the tenseness of the situation.

"My dear chap, you should cough or scrape your feet before coming into a lady's room at so late an hour."

Madame Pompé withdrew her bare arms from around Wentworth's neck and stepped back from him, turning her gaze toward the newcomer. Even in those few seconds she regained control of herself. She surveyed the intruder with a magnificent portrayal of outward calm, but she *was* exercising control. She appeared to be studying the man with the guns, trying to read his mind through the mask.

Wentworth believed that he was in the presence of the criminal he had sought so long; yet he watched the woman while she watched the man. During those few seconds he noted the slight stiffness of her delicate nostrils and knew that she was acting, that her calm exterior cloaked anxiety. He knew that she had been filled with fear just before she broke away from him and that now she was masterfully controlling it. He wished to know the cause of that fear. He waited.

"My dear, you have done very well, except that it was scarcely necessary for you to embrace him." The man had become quite as cool as Wentworth. "I found that the police had withdrawn from this building, and I thought I would come up and see how you were getting along—not that the police could have kept me away if I had really needed to come."

Wentworth's keen eyes noticed the slight relaxation which came over Madame Pompé as the man finished speaking. She no longer needed to exercise control over herself. She was at her ease, and Wentworth knew what he wanted to know.

His deduction was so quick that it must have been intuitive as well as mental. It was quite obvious that she had relaxed because of the newcomer's friendly speech to her and that she had not been expecting him. There could then have been but one reason for her sudden fear. She had not known how much of her conversation the masked man had overheard, and she had been terrified lest he had heard her suggestion that Wentworth should take her away. Apparently she had been at least partly genuine in the proposition.

"I suppose you know me, Mr.—ah—" commenced Wentworth and stopped.

"Most certainly, my very dear Mr. Richard Wentworth," was the cool and almost drawling rejoinder. "As for me, suppose I choose a *nom de guerre,* a war name. Suppose that you call me Mr. X during the very few minutes that you have yet to live."

"*Merci mille fois,* Monsieur X," replied Wentworth suavely. "I give you a thousand thanks for your very great courtesy."

"*Ii n'y a pas de quoi,* my very dear Richard Wentworth. It is nothing at all and no thanks are necessary. You are quite a difficult man to kill, and I really think that I should thank you. Most men are so very easy to kill. There is no pleasure in it at all."

"At our last encounter, if I remember correctly," remarked Wentworth calmly, "you did me the honor of running away from me. Perhaps you will do so again—if I let you. By the way, you might do me a very small favor before I—ah—die."

"And what may that be?"

"You might inform me why you are wearing a glove on your left hand, but none on your right."

Mr. X did not reply, but something which sounded like a snarl came from behind his mask.

"Touched you, eh?"

Again the snarl sounded behind the mask, so definitely threatening that Madame Pompé started nervously and dropped her handkerchief.

WENTWORTH STOOPED slowly and picked the fallen bit of linen from the floor. He held it idly in his fingers while he leaned upon the mantelpiece and watched the man with the two guns. Although he appeared carelessly calm, he was really studying his opponent minutely to determine the last moment before which he would have to take some kind of action if he were to continue living.

"I am very highly complimented, my very dear Mr. X, that you should consider it necessary to bring *two* pistols with which to kill me. I fear, however, that you will use neither of them."

"Indeed? Why not?"

Wentworth raised the handkerchief to his nose for a second and dropped the tiny piece of lace upon the mantelpiece with a careless motion. The action brought him a trifle nearer to his opera hat which stood upon the far end of the mantelpiece and which held his small revolver.

"Excellent perfume, my dear Corinne." He indicated the handkerchief on the mantelpiece, and took a short step nearer his hat.

Mr. X chuckled behind his mask and knocked the opera hat to the floor with the barrel of one of his pistols. "You are very clever, my dear Richard Wentworth," he remarked smoothly as the little revolver was jarred from its elastic loops and slid out into plain view upon the floor, "but you are not quite a match for me!"

"I think you have come to the end, Mr. Wentworth," said Madame Pompé, shrugging her magnificent shoulders. "If you can get out of this jam, you will go even higher in my estimation."

"Excellent, my dear Corinne," returned Wentworth easily. "I shall show you how the trick can be turned."

"You will have to turn it rather quickly, my friend," remarked Mr. X, commencing to raise the pistol in his right hand. "Nobody will hear this shot, up here on the roof of this apartment building—not even you! The bullet will reach your forehead before the sound reaches your ears."

Madame Pompé turned her eyes away to avoid the sight of what was to happen.

"I wouldn't do that, Mr. X," Wentworth said a trifle quickly, but without any emotion. "You will be dead in another second if you continue."

Wentworth's voice had not been raised in the slightest above normal, but the words were spoken with so much quiet assurance that Mr. X lowered his pistol a little and flashed one swift glance about the room.

"Is bluff the only weapon you have left, my friend?" he asked. "I am afraid that you cannot bluff me."

"Then let me show you something that will surprise you," Wentworth said.

From the mantelpiece the tall and indolent man raised Madame Pompé's tiny handkerchief. He reached upward and tucked a corner of the piece of cambric under the frame of a picture which hung over the mantel, so that the handkerchief was suspended against the wall well above his head. There was a trace of a smile on his lips as he faced Mr. X again.

"A strange proceeding," commented Mr. X, apparently interested.

"Quite! You will find it very strange indeed if you will be so good as to watch closely."

Madame Pompé was watching Wentworth very intently and curiously. Slowly she sank into a chair and assumed a posture for the benefit of the strange man who was doing such an apparently absurd thing with her handkerchief. Madame Pompé never forgot that she was a woman.

"You really must explain yourself a little more intelligently," Mr. X insisted.

"I shall be glad to explain," replied Wentworth. "Since you came into this room, my dear Mr. X, I have always been in a position to kill you instantly. Even if you had tried to shoot me, it is exceedingly doubtful if you could have fired quickly enough. If you had been successful you, yourself, would have been dying before you could have lowered your pistol again."

MR. X bent a little toward Wentworth as though trying to scrutinize him through the holes in his mask.

"I shall give you half a minute to prove your words, Wentworth," Mr. X challenged incisively.

"Very well," Wentworth returned with easy assurance. "Come and stand in front of the handkerchief. I want you to watch it closely."

Mr. X moved slowly around Wentworth and faced the handkerchief where it hung upon the wall, its corner pinned by the picture frame. He was wise enough, however, not to come within reach of Wentworth's long arms. A man can be disarmed by an expert, if he comes within striking distance.

"Ready?" asked Wentworth, still leaning carelessly against the mantelpiece.

"Yes, I am ready," was the cold reply.

"Good!" returned Wentworth. "Now watch me closely. I am going to point my finger at that handkerchief—just as I could have pointed it at you, Mr. X, at any moment since you came into this room."

Slowly Wentworth began to raise his right arm, with fist closed, toward the handkerchief.

Mr. X watched the slow movement of the arm keenly. His eyes darted from Wentworth to the handkerchief and back again to Wentworth. His arms hung loosely, the two pistols pointing downward, triggers slightly pressed and ready for action if necessary.

Madame Pompé struck a match and watched Wentworth intently through the first puff of smoke from her cigarette. She was no longer posing for him. She was admiring him, almost openly, notwithstanding the presence of the masked man who held two pistols ready for action.

Wentworth's ascending arm came into alignment with the handkerchief and halted. From his fist the index finger shot out. Something flashed through the air, directly above the head of Mr. X, and a heavy knife struck the wall, pinning a corner of the handkerchief. Broken plaster spattered upon the mantelpiece, but the knife struck so hard that it remained imbedded in the wall.

The effect was dramatic, far more so than a pistol shot would have been. It hinted a further outcome which might be horribly tragic.

But the nerve of Mr. X was splendid. He neither started nor attempted to turn his head, although the knife had come through the open window from directly behind him.

Madame Pompé, too, was cool. But she stopped smoking and her eyes showed her admiration as she continued to regard Wentworth.

"If you make any move, my very dear Mr. X," remarked Wentworth, "or if you fail to drop your pistols to the floor, the next knife will strike between your shoulder blades."

From among the potted plants on the roof Ram Singh stepped through the open window. Another knife, held by the naked blade in his upraised hand, was poised to throw.

The pistol in the left hand of Mr. X thudded upon the floor.

"Thank you, my very dear Mr. X," said Wentworth, still leaning carelessly against the mantelpiece. "I would like the other pistol, now, if you please."

Suddenly the masked man staggered. He clutched at his heart with his left hand. He swayed and his knees gave way. Just as he sank, apparently in agony, upon the floor he fired his other pistol—straight into the wall to one side of the mantelpiece!

The room was plunged into darkness. Mr. X had fired into the wall-switch and short circuited the lights!

CHAPTER 12
WENTWORTH TASTES FEAR

THE LAST second of light had presented a particularly dramatic scene. The great criminal, sinisterly masked, appeared to be collapsing in agony upon the floor. Behind him the huge Hindu stood with knife poised, ready to throw or to spring. To one side, still leaning against the mantelpiece, Richard Wentworth regarded the scene calmly, master of the situation up to that moment. Madame Pompé forgot to smoke, forgot to pose for masculine eyes, stared in admiration at the man by the mantelpiece.

Then came the pistol shot and darkness. There was the thud of steel striking wood and, in the very dim light from the open window, the figure of Ram Singh could be seen bounding forward.

Swiftly Wentworth drew a flashlight from his pocket and shot a beam of light to the spot upon which the mysterious Mr. X had stood. There, with point deeply imbedded in the polished floor, was the Hindu's second knife and Ram Singh, himself,

Ram Singh stepped through the open window, another knife held by naked blade....

crouched above it in the attitude of seizing something which was no longer there.

Mr. X had vanished.

Even while Wentworth pointed the flashlight at the knife in the floor, he snapped his lighter with the other hand and ignited several ornamental candles which stood upon the mantelpiece. In the soft light the black portières swayed and bulged into the room a little.

Ram Singh, noticing the movement of the portières, sprang into them with arms outstretched to seize what stood behind. His weight tore one of the portières from its rings and he went to the floor with it. There was a muffled scream, and the Hindu staggered back into the room, carrying something which wriggled within the portière.

From one end of his bundle a black-stockinged leg protruded. From the other end could be seen the tousled head of Mimi. He brought what he had found to Wentworth, like a dog bringing something to his master. But the look on his face was one of disgust when only Mimi emerged.

Wentworth picked up his revolver from the floor, where Mr. X had brazenly allowed it to remain, and left Ram Singh with the two women while he rapidly searched the penthouse. He did not expect to find his man. But when dealing with such an audacious person he felt that precautions were necessary. Undoubtedly Mr. X had escaped by the emergency stairs, there having been no time to call an elevator to the top of the building.

To follow him would have been difficult, and Wentworth had something else in view.

Ram Singh was squatting on the floor when his master returned to the front room. In his hand the native held the great knife which he had drawn out of the floor. Mimi, restless and nervous, stood beside her mistress. Madame Pompé smoked with apparent indifference.

"That will be all, Mimi," said Wentworth. "You may go to bed."

"*Mais Madame?*" queried the girl, surprised and looking toward her mistress.

"You heard me, Mimi!" Wentworth said sharply. "I am sorry for the little accident at the portières. Please accept my apology. Now get out!"

The apology was a $20 bill which Wentworth took from his

pocketbook, allowing that pocketbook to fall open so that much more money could be seen by both maid and mistress.

"*Merci, Monsieur!*" exclaimed the maid enthusiastically and withdrew with a question to her mistress over her shoulder. "Madame will ring for her bath in the morning?"

The question was really a statement of what Mimi expected would happen. She did not understand the situation, but she saw that her mistress did not wish her to remain and—Mimi was French.

To Ram Singh, Wentworth spoke again in Hindustani, and that very earnest servant disappeared once more through the open window, taking his great knife with him.

MADAME POMPÉ'S eyes were half closed, dreamy and thoughtful, as she watched her very unusual companion for a moment or two after they were alone. The candle light robbed her of the slight hardness which strong light made visible on her face. She was certainly very beautiful, a beautiful animal perhaps. And she had nerve, plenty of it.

Wentworth filled the two glasses with champagne again and handed one of them to her. He raised his own glass.

"I shall give you a toast," he said. "To Mr. X, the cleverest criminal I have ever met. May we meet again very soon!"

"I hate him!" she exclaimed, glancing toward the hall a little fearfully.

"You need not be afraid," he said. "My boy is on guard outside, and he can see into the hall through the open window."

"What do you want?" she asked flatly.

Wentworth went to the little table without replying and took

119

the remaining bottle of wine from the basket which Ram Singh had brought. He felt its temperature thoughtfully and placed it upon the table, unopened.

"I shall tell you want I want, Corinne," he said, resuming his seat beside her.

"Yes?" she inquired impatiently as he paused. "What?"

"I want you to tell me the real name of Mr. X."

She shivered. "I couldn't!" she exclaimed. "You might fail, and then he would cut my heart out!"

"Then you *do* know who he really is," Wentworth commented significantly. "I was a little bit afraid that you might not know his real name."

"I didn't say I did," retorted Madame Pompé quickly. "He uses several names. How do I know which one is his real one?"

"You know it very well, my dear Corinne," he returned. "I can read women as easily as you can read men. You are going to tell me the real name of Mr. X."

"No!" she protested. "I am afraid. I would have left him long ago if I had not been terrified of him. I dare not do it."

"There is nothing to be afraid of. The police will lock him up in no time."

"No! No! No! No lawyer could convict him. If he did, the police could never hold such a man."

"But I could kill him."

She looked at him, her eyes large, and nodded her head as if afraid to speak the thought aloud.

"Then tell me his name."

"I will on one condition and on one condition only," she returned emphatically.

"The condition?"

"I will tell you his name in Europe after you take me there safely," she answered. "After that you can return to New York and do what you like with him."

"Thank you Corinne," said Wentworth, reaching to the table and carelessly placing the wicker wine basket upon his knees. "That would be very kind of you but, unfortunately, I must have the name in 24 hours."

She shook her head violently. "Impossible! I would rather die!"

"Then, my dear lady, you will have to die," said Wentworth quietly.

MADAME POMPÉ looked at him sharply, startled. "What do you mean?" she asked, her voice not quite steady.

"In the bottom half of this wicker basket," he explained, "there is a voice-recording apparatus. It is a very beautiful piece of mechanical construction. The motor runs in oil and is quite soundless. I started the motor when I took the second bottle out of the basket, and our last conversation is completely recorded. Just a minute... I shall have the little machine reproduce it for you."

Wentworth replaced the basket upon the table and watched her with the unemotional interest that a scientist might have for the contents of a test tube.

Madame Pompé leaned back in her chair, clutching its arms and trying to remember exactly what she had said.

There was some silence, then the little machine spoke:

"You know it very well, my dear Corinne. I can read women as easily as you can read men. You are going to tell me the real name of Mr. X."… "No! I am afraid. I would have left him long ago if I had not been terrified of him. I dare not do it."

Madame Pompé heard her own rich voice, mingled with that of Wentworth, as the machine began to retrace the recent conversation. She sat motionless and silent while her face became more and more strained.

The conversation continued: "Then tell me his name."… "I will on one condition and on one condition only."… "The condition?"… "I will tell you his name in Europe after you take me there safely. After that you can return to New York and do what you like with him."

"Well?" asked Wentworth, reaching into the basket and stopping the motor abruptly. "Shall I take steps to see that Mr. X receives this record of our conversation? I rather think that he would be interested in your offer to betray him."

Madame Pompé sprang to her feet, aflame with rage and fear. Furious and trembling she stood before him, at a loss for words, while he remained calmly seated.

"Of course you need have no fear, Corinne," he said, "if you give me the name."

Suddenly she lifted her handbag. And he saw that in her right hand pressed against the bag's side and shielded by it from view through the open window, was the little pistol which she had shown him earlier that evening. The deadly weapon was leveled straight at Wentworth's heart, and her finger was tightening slowly about the trigger!

Wentworth reached to the table and took up his glass of wine. He raised it and smiled at her over its brim. "A charming picture," he said.

"Give me the record, or I shoot," she warned, in a voice too low to be heard through the open window.

"Think twice," he warned indifferently. "An ugly knife will tear through your charming breast before I strike the floor."

She was woman to the last. "Is it charming?" she asked, hesitating.

"My dear," he answered, sipping his wine, "it is superb."

"If you really thought so you would not make me kill you," she retorted in the same low voice. "I've *got* to do it. I could not stand the torture that *he* would put me through before I died."

Wentworth continued to sip the wine. It was distinctly a novel situation to face a woman intent upon killing him. He continued to smile slightly at her over his glass.

AS IN the case of most women, her eyes partly closed as she pulled the trigger. There was a harmless click, and Madame Pompé collapsed into her chair.

"My dear Corinne," Wentworth said as he picked up her wine glass and offered it to her, "you really should be more observant. I removed the cartridges from the magazine of your pistol before I handed it back to you."

Madame Pompé took the glass and drained it. She leaned back in her chair and looked at him. There was fear in her eyes, and anger—and admiration.

Very firmly and with cold finality Wentworth assured her that Mr. X would receive the record of her voice, if she did not divulge that mysterious man's real name. He convinced her that, sooner or later, he must meet his enemy again and that, upon that occasion, he would make it his first business to give the evidence of her contemplated treachery to the man she feared. On the other hand he promised her full protection if she did as he wished.

Finally Madame Pompé, in apparent desperation, agreed to divulge the name at Wentworth's apartment on the following night, provided he would take her under his protection until Mr. X was captured.

It was then that the telephone bell sounded. Wentworth picked up the instrument and answered before Madame Pompé could move.

The cold, sardonic voice of Mr. X came to him over the wire. Mr. X expressed himself as being delighted that Mr. Wentworth was still visiting with the charming lady but wondered if there might not be another lady whom he was neglecting.

Wentworth, uneasy at the mention of another lady and his mind immediately reverting to Nita, forced himself to reply indifferently that there were many ladies who possessed great attraction and that he could not be with them all at the same time.

From the other end of the wire the cold, cutting voice continued. Wentworth was informed that he would feel the power of Mr. X in a very few minutes.

"It was only necessary for me to be quite certain of your exact location, my dear Mr. Wentworth, before I struck." Mr. X stated.

"Unless you can strike over the telephone, I am afraid that you have not the courage to strike at all," was Wentworth's quiet taunt.

"I shall have much pleasure in striking both over the telephone and in person," replied Mr. X. "I should advise you not to forget the other lady while you wait the few minutes that will be required for me to arrive."

The telephone connection was broken at the other end before Wentworth could reply. He looked at Madame Pompé. She was nervously smoking. A light breeze came through the open window, causing the candles on the mantelpiece to flicker. An electric light in the hall, unharmed by the fuse which had been blown, threw some of its steady light into the front room because of the portière which had been torn down.

Everything seemed quiet and without any sign of danger. Yet Wentworth felt certain that Mr. X would not weaken his reputation by means of a senseless bluff. Something was going to happen and happen quickly.

ABRUPTLY WENTWORTH picked up the telephone again and dialed his own number. The mention of another woman had hinted a danger far greater than any personal threat to himself could possibly be.

The sleepy voice of a maid on duty came to him after a short wait.

"This is Mr. Wentworth speaking. Waken Miss Van Sloan and ask her to take the phone."

125

"Miss Van Sloan has gone out, sir," the sleepy voice of the maid replied.

"Gone out?" The query was shot over the wire like a bullet. His hand gripped the telephone until the knuckles went white. "Where did she go?"

"I don't know, sir. She went out a few minutes after you telephoned. I think she said she was going to meet you, sir."

"I telephoned? But I didn't telephone."

"Excuse me, sir, but you did. I answered the telephone, and you asked for Miss Van Sloan just like you did now, sir. I recognized your voice at once."

This blow, and it came to him over the telephone, was greater than any Richard Wentworth had ever received. That Nita had been decoyed from his apartment could not be doubted. In that fraction of a second the room swayed before the eyes of the mentally anguished man at the telephone. Had his passion for excitement and danger brought disaster to the one woman he really loved?

Then his mind cleared. He saw Madame Pompé watching him intently, smoking mechanically. Through the open window came a strangled cry, a cry of warning or a cry for help.

Wentworth crashed the telephone upon the table and sprang to the window, peering out while his flashlight shot here and there among the potted plants. The beam fell upon Ram Singh, lying upon the roof.

Reckless of hidden danger among the potted plants, Wentworth leaped through the window and knelt beside his servant, supporting the turbaned head on his arm while he spoke urgently in Hindustani in an endeavor to bring the man back to full consciousness.

It was the great turban which had saved Ram Singh from death. He had been struck on top of the head by some person who had crept up behind him while he stood on guard at the window.

In two or three minutes the servant was able to sit up. He adjusted his turban and assured his master that he was all right and quite ready to stick his knife into his enemy if he could only find him.

Wentworth turned to the open window. The candles on the mantelpiece had been extinguished, and the light in the hall was no longer burning. The penthouse was in complete darkness.

Under ordinary circumstances, circumstances which did not bring danger to the woman he loved, Wentworth would have used subtlety. He would have moved slowly and with great cunning. But with Nita in danger, he was forced to cast all caution aside.

FOLLOWED BY Ram Singh, he went through the window in a rush, his flashlight circling the room as he entered. The room was empty. Madame Pompé had gone, and she had taken with her the wicker wine basket containing the incriminating evidence of her spoken words. It seemed as though Mr. X was striking back successfully at Wentworth, defeating him, driving him into a corner.

Almost desperate, Wentworth decided instantly that it was necessary for him to run away. For Nita's sake he could not remain to continue the fight any longer.

With Ram Singh he darted into the hall and found the electric switch. He turned it. There was no light. He came to the front door which opened upon the elevator. The elevator hall was also dark, and no light came up the elevator shaft. He pressed the bell to call the car. No car responded. Faint sounds of confusion ascended to him through the empty shaft. It seemed as though the electric current, both for power and light, had been cut off from the entire building.

For Wentworth to gain the street it would be necessary to descend twenty flights of stairs through a pitch black building. On every landing a man might be lurking behind a partly opened door, waiting with pistol raised or with strangling cord looped. Yet Wentworth did not consider the risk to himself, but only the risk to Nita if he failed to reach the street alive.

He threw open the door to the stairs and was about to begin the perilous descent when he faintly heard the ringing of the telephone in the front room of the penthouse. Instantly he rushed back and picked up the receiver—just as Madame Pompé, emerging from a bedroom, was about to take it.

The whole world changed for Richard Wentworth as he held the telephone to his ear. He was no longer troubled by thoughts of sudden death. He could laugh at all people and all things once more.

It was Nita's voice, and she was laughing.

She told him that she had heard his voice on the telephone, at least that she thought that it was his voice, asking her to meet him alone in Central Park at once. She had responded of course, but she had taken Apollo with her.

In the park she had been seized by a strange man. But her attacker had not expected Apollo. He was, she said, probably still running, minus half a sleeve which Apollo had insisted upon bringing back to the apartment.

Wentworth laughed in pure joy at the knowledge of her safety. "But how did you get my telephone number?" he asked.

"The police had your last call traced," she answered.

"Good old New York police!" he exclaimed. "I am coming home as soon as they get the elevator running again in this building."

"What are you doing in a lady's penthouse at this hour of the morning?"

"Tell you later," he replied with a chuckle, and hung up.

CHAPTER 13
SPARKS REPORTS

WENTWORTH DID not want to use the power of the police upon Madame Pompé. He needed the information she could give him regarding the identity of the criminal he sought. But he was afraid that any such attempt might cause his quarry to take flight for some considerable length of time. He knew only too well that the man who styled himself Mr. X was a master of cunning and could only be defeated in desperate encounter or by means of the most cautious planning.

There was another avenue of information which Wentworth wished to explore before probing further in any other direction.

He wished to know why this master criminal wanted to get in touch with Jack Selwyn, the confidential clerk of the diamond merchant.

Without thought of sleep Wentworth, accompanied by Ram Singh, returned to the Park Avenue apartment where Wentworth changed to day clothes and set out immediately upon his search for Selwyn.

Day was just breaking when he came to the address given him by Dorothy Canfield and found a very cheap apartment building upon the west side of town. There was a narrow entrance sandwiched between a tobacconist and a barber shop. The front door was ajar, and he entered the tiny, dismally lighted hall with its usual clutter of rickety letter boxes. Nobody was in sight and he quickly found the letter box bearing the name of George Baker, the false name used by the man he was seeking. It required only a few seconds for him to ascend the narrow stairs and arrive at the Baker room on the third floor.

Without knocking, Wentworth threw open the door and entered. A single glance showed him that the room was empty. It was poorly furnished, and the bed was badly rumpled, showing that it had been slept in. Abruptly Wentworth bent forward, playing his flashlight over the bed. Upon the sheet were several large drops of blood. He touched one of the red spots with his finger, and it came away red. The blood was very fresh.

Richard Wentworth seldom allowed himself to show emotion in moments of surprise or stress, but he sat now upon a chair and stared at the bed with a frowning, troubled face. He did not know Jack Selwyn, who now called himself George Baker.

He had only known Dorothy Canfield during a few minutes of conversation, but he had taken her under his protection and he visioned her pathetic face at the news that her sweetheart's bed was covered with fresh blood, her sweetheart vanished.

The troubled frowning disappeared from his face and, for a moment, was replaced by an expression of ferocity that was almost shocking. Then the ferocity, too, faded away and he swung around on his chair, cool but inexorably determined.

HIS EYES swept the room and on the floor he noticed a photograph which, on examination, proved to be that of a very good looking young man. He turned the photograph over and found the name and address of George Baker written upon the back, the address being complete even to the number of the room which now contained the blood-stained sheet.

The handwriting was that of a woman and, so far as Wentworth could remember, it was that of Dorothy Canfield. Slipping the photograph into his pocket he left the room, almost running into a woman with a mop and bucket in the hall.

"Know where Mr. Baker works?" he asked, not expecting that she did.

"Sure!" she answered. "He works for the tobacconist down-stairs."

The tobacconist, who also sold newspapers, was just opening his store in the early morning light.

"Seen Baker lately?" Wentworth asked as he came out on the street.

"He's gone to the doctor to see a sick friend," the tobacconist replied. "Found a note from him pinned on my door when I arrived this morning."

"What doctor?" snapped Wentworth.

"Don't know. Here's the note… You can read it for yourself."

Wentworth took the note. It had been scribbled very rapidly on the back of an envelope and read: "Gone to doctor to see a sick friend. Back as soon as she is better."

The tobacconist knew nothing more. Wentworth raised his stick and stopped a night-prowling taxi on its way to its garage. Soon he was whirling across Central Park once more on his way to Park Avenue where people sleep much later than they do in that part of the west side which he had just left.

At his apartment Wentworth sent the maid on duty to awaken Miss Van Sloan. She came swiftly to him in the dining room where he was drinking coffee and eating several rashers of bacon broiled by Jenkyns himself upon the sideboard. She was dressed in a turquoise wrapper of Chinese silk and her hair hung loose over her shoulders.

"By Jove!" he exclaimed, waiving Jenkyns out of the room. "Nita, you look prettier when you get up than when you go to bed. You are one of nature's miracles."

Her face glowed with pleasure at the compliment, but worry overtook it. "What is it, Dick?" she asked. "What has happened?"

"It's little Dorothy," he answered, "and it's bad. They got her sweetheart and I'm afraid he's been done in."

"Oh!" She sank trembling into a chair by his side. "I—I was afraid it was you. Poor little girl! But I'm glad you are all right, Dick."

"Tut, tut!" he chided, pouring her a cup of coffee. "I'm a tough old bird. You shouldn't worry about me."

Then he explained to her what had happened. "The trouble is," he continued, "I simply must question the girl, and it is going to be difficult not to drive her crazy with fear."

"Poor little girl," Nita repeated sympathetically. "She will have to know some time, Dick."

IN A few minutes Nita brought Dorothy Canfield to the breakfast table for a cup of coffee and a talk with Wentworth. She, too, was very pretty. But it was the charm of youth shining in her eyes and not the poetry of the soul as in the case of Nita.

"Dorothy," began Wentworth, "you will remember that you wrote your sweetheart's address for me in the music room and that I burned it after reading it. Now I want you to think very hard. Did you ever write that address at any other time?"

Dorothy puckered her face in thought, then shook her head in the negative.

Wentworth took the photograph out of his pocket and placed it beside her, face up. "Did you leave this in your room?"

"Oh yes!" she exclaimed. "I left it under the mattress where I always kept it hidden."

Wentworth turned it over, exposing the written address. "And did you write on the back of it?"

Dorothy crimsoned. "Ye-es," she admitted. "I forgot that I had written the address on the back of it. It was when Jack first telephoned the address to me and I was afraid that I might forget it."

"My dear," he reproved her, "you should not have done that.

133

Suppose that your enemy had searched your room and found it. He would have had Jack Selwyn, now known as Mr. George Baker, completely at his mercy. And that might have prevented their ever being any Mr. and Mrs. Selwyn or even any Mr. and Mrs. Baker."

"But he didn't!" she exclaimed vehemently. "He didn't find it! Tell me that he didn't!"

"Of course not, my dear," lied Wentworth smilingly. "I am very glad that I found it. Now, tell me something more. Has your Jack any relatives in New York or very close friends, people to whom he might entrust his new name?"

She shook her head decisively. "He has no relatives at all in New York, and he told his new name only to me."

Wentworth looked very grave when Dorothy went back to bed for some more sleep. "Nita, there isn't much hope," he said. "It is plain that Selwyn was traced by the photograph with the address upon it which Dorothy left in her room. It also seems certain that he has no friend who would send for him in case of accident or illness—except Dorothy herself. The only deduction is that he was decoyed, probably told that Dorothy was hurt or sick. However, if that is true, I cannot understand the reason for the blood on the sheet. There seems to be only one other possibility and that is that he was forcibly abducted and made to write the note for the tobacconist to prevent any quick inquiry regarding his absence from work."

Nita's hand stole into his. "It almost makes you sick to let a thing like this happen, doesn't it?" she asked. "Is it your heart or your pride?"

"Both," he said, "and something more—my hatred for defeat." Unexpectedly he struck the table such a blow with his fist that the coffee cups rattled and the girl started violently. "By God, Nita, I'll smash somebody for this."

Jenkyns, the butler, came silently into the dining room with a portable telephone in his hand. He came so silently that Nita did not notice and left her hand in Wentworth's grasp.

"Beg pardon, sir, but there is a telephone call for you."

"Who is it, Jenkyns?"

"The—ah—person, sir, will not give his name and I might say, sir, that the individual is very much intoxicated. Oh, very intoxicated, indeed, sir!"

"Plug it in, Jenkyns," said Wentworth, taking the telephone while the butler stooped to plug the end of the cord into the wall connection. "Hello!... Shut up, you young fool and talk slowly... You have been in fifteen speakeasies?... Why did you stop? There are some more, you know... Oh, is that you, Sparks? What the devil have you been doing?... Been arrested for carrying my rapier stick? You blighter! I want that stick back... You ran it into the stern of a drunken radio announcer in the fifteenth speakeasy? Never do such a thing, my boy, except in the first ten speakeasies. After that it's dangerous."

For awhile Wentworth listened to more babbling over the wire and made no reply. Then, suddenly, he became vitally interested.

"You say that Madame Pompé was running around with a certain medical doctor just before she gave up radio singing?... Yes, yes! Say that again... Madame Pompé was traveling the great white way with Dr. Sylvester Quornelle? Is that the name...? Excellent! Where are you now?... In some police station? You don't know where but you think it's in New York? I'll see what I can do for you. How severely did you wound this radio announcer?... He's pinched too, and he can't sit down? Well, I'll see what I can do for you... What's that? The *Molly Ann* is lighted up and they are carrying big metal cylinders on board?... Good work, old man! Get some sleep."

Wentworth tossed the portable telephone to the butler like an English drill sergeant tossing a rifle to a recruit. He strode out of the room, almost dragging Nita to her feet in forgetfulness that he yet held her hand.

"A drunken reporter, named Sparks," he told the inspector, "has just run a rapier into the rear of a drunken radio announcer, name unknown. Both are so drunk that they do not know what police station they are in. I would consider it a favor if you would bring them both up here for questioning, inspector."

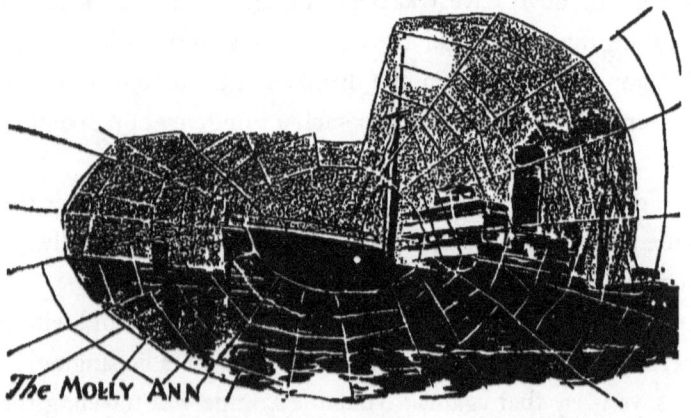

The MOLLY ANN

"All right!" the inspector grinned. "And may I ask where you are going, Mr. Wentworth? You seem always to be some place or going somewhere."

"I am going after the greatest, living criminal, my dear inspector, a man who will shock the world if we do not stop him in a very few hours. There seems to be no limit to his audacity—nor to his cruelty."

CHAPTER 14
THE DARK HOUSE

RICHARD WENTWORTH was not one to give up while the least trace of hope remained. It was this trait which had kept him alive upon many desperate occasions and which, at times, had brought him success amid overwhelming difficulties. The mention of a doctor as the friend of Madame Pompé gave him a faint hope that he might yet be able to rescue the man upon whom Dorothy Canfield depended for her happiness. Jack Selwyn's note to the tobacconist had stated that he was going to a doctor. If this doctor proved to be Dr. Sylvester Quornelle, much could and would be done.

Dr. Quornelle lived within a few blocks of Wentworth's Park Avenue apartment, just off Fifth Avenue. Wentworth found the address in the telephone book, and straightway dialed a medical friend, who was at that moment asleep and dreaming.

"This is Richard Wentworth."

"Dick Wentworth? You are never sick. What the devil do you mean by waking me up in the middle of the night?"

"The sun is up and the robins are pulling worms on the golf course. Tell me what you know about Dr. Quornelle."

"Sylvester Quornelle? Don't know much of anything about him. But I believe that he was a rather clever alienist. Had a theory that all bodily ailments came from diseases of the mind. He disappeared a couple of years ago. I think he went to Europe to study. Your mind going back on you?"

"Must be or I wouldn't call up such a blithering idiot for information. Shoot you some golf next week."

The information seemed to be significant and very interesting, when related to the other slight details which Wentworth knew about the man he was hunting. Of course Dr. Sylvester Quornelle might be perfectly innocent and quite unconnected with crime. But Wentworth decided that he must investigate.

His first act was to survey Dr. Quornelle's residence from the street. To do this he took Apollo for his morning walk and strolled slowly past the address which he had found in the telephone book, apparently only interested in the great dog and enjoying the leisurely exercise of his early morning walk.

Dr. Quornelle's home proved to be a fairly large house of evident value. Doors and windows were completely boarded over, and it seemed as though it had not been lived in for a long time. The fact that Dr. Quornelle's telephone was still listed did not mean anything, since many wealthy owners maintained their telephones while absent, for the use of caretakers in case of emergency.

Wentworth was not satisfied. He quickened his steps and returned to his apartment, determined to investigate more certainly. From a locked cabinet in his bedroom he took a remarkably thin leather case which he strapped to his side underneath his vest. The case was so thin that his coat hung over it without giving any evidence of its presence. Inside the case was a set of chrome steel tools which would have made any burglar envious. From the same cabinet he also took a bunch of delicate keys some one of which would, in his expert fingers, open any ordinary lock. He also placed in his pocket the new air pistol, one of the few air weapons ever made to have high-power penetration.

Richard Wentworth was well prepared when he started out the second time, now without the dog. He was well prepared, but it required more than preparation to burglarize a residence on a fashionable New York street in broad daylight. It required, also, the amazing daring and quick resourcefulness with which Wentworth was so well equipped. In the interest of what he considered to be justice he was about to break the law by forcibly entering another man's home. If caught he would have no defense save, perhaps, his wit.

IT WAS still very early morning in fashionable New York when Wentworth again approached the house of Dr. Quornelle. Few people were astir and the street was almost bare. He was reading a newspaper as he arrived at the house and he turned into the tradesman entrance without ceasing to read the paper, quite as if he had a perfect right to go where he was going. A bold approach was much better than a crafty approach in daylight. He knew that it was taking a chance, but the risk, he believed, was comparatively small. And in any event it was taking chances which afforded him most of his interest in life.

The door for tradespeople was unboarded, which might mean that it was being used by a caretaker. Wentworth had no difficulty with the lock, which yielded to one of his keys almost immediately. He entered and closed the door, locking it behind him. The locked door might interfere with a rapid escape, but an unlocked door might warn somebody of the presence of an intruder. It was dark inside and he stood very still, listening and even smelling, but there was nothing to hear, and the musty smell seemed natural under the circumstances.

After a pause he moved forward and used his flashlight sparingly, noticing the usual basement arrangements. As he was about to ascend the stairs, he noticed a door at the rear of the basement. Testing it, he was surprised to find that it was unlocked. He opened it slightly and found that it gave upon a small back yard. This, thought Wentworth, was most unusual. Why should this door be unlocked?

He studied the back yard through the partly opened portal and saw a door in the wall of the yard—a door which must open into the back yard of the adjacent building. Here then was an undercover means of exit from and entrance to the house with the boarded windows.

Wentworth closed the back door thoughtfully. He had found the first slight indication that things were not as they seemed in the Quornelle house. It was quite possible that he was not alone in the building.

He ascended the stairs very quietly and emerged in the

kitchen as he had expected. But here he found more evidence of life. The kitchen window, overlooking the back yard, was not boarded. Pilot flames were burning in the gas stove and a half filled coffee pot was still warm.

Swiftly but carefully Wentworth peered into the front rooms of the first floor. They were almost completely dark because of the boarded windows at the front of the house. Furniture showed dim and ghostly in white coverings. At the entrance to a large room at the front of the house a moth, disturbed by his presence, brushed his face. But he stood perfectly still in the deep gloom, not starting in the slightest. It was well that he did so.

From the top of the broad stairs, leading to the floor above, a beam of light shot downward. Wentworth leaned slowly backward into the folds of a heavy portière which hung at the entrance to the large front room.

The light from above vanished, and there came the soft tread of a man descending the heavily carpeted stairs. He came slowly and stepped irregularly, as if he were slightly lame. He passed so close to the entrance of the front room that Wentworth could hear him breathing but it was too dark to see his face or even to note his figure distinctly.

Without using his flashlight again, and evidently quite familiar with the house, the man turned to the rear, and Wentworth heard him opening the door which led to the basement.

It was a natural conclusion that the unknown man was about to leave the house by way of the rear door in the basement. Rapidly Wentworth returned to the kitchen and cautiously peered through the window into the back yard. But his view of the gate in the wall was cut off by a jutting bay window. He descended swiftly, but with the caution of a cat, into the basement and found that the rear door had been locked. Somebody had used the door since he had left it. Once more Wentworth ascended to the first floor and stood in the dark at the foot of the main stairway. He believed now that he was alone in the house, but he could not be certain. His feet touched the thick covering of the stairs very, very gently as he ascended to the floor above.

At the top of the stairs Wentworth found himself in a hall almost as large as the one he had left. There were doors on both sides leading to bedrooms and a library. The furniture of the bedrooms was white covered, and the beds showed no sign of recent use. There was a locked door at the back of the house which interested the investigator. But not knowing how much time he might have, he turned his attention first to the library.

Wentworth threw his flashlight over the backs of the books and found most of them to be either medical or scientific. He was examining an ash tray with fresh ashes in it when he stopped to sniff. He had detected at that moment a slight odor of chemicals.

IT IS difficult to trace the source of a slight smell in a room; it is almost impossible to discover that source in a dark room fitfully exposed by a wandering flashlight. But Wentworth was extremely thorough when he was at work. What he did not know, he fought to learn. Finally he decided that the faint smell of chemicals was issuing from what seemed to be a large box or chest covered with a rich drapery. This piece of furniture was not in harmony with the remainder of the room, and Wentworth surveyed it critically.

Lifting the drapery carefully, he exposed a large iron safe; and the faint chemical smell became a trifle more distinct. A moth fell out of the drapes and lay upon the floor under the beam from his flashlight. He smiled indulgently at sight of the old-fashioned combination lock of the safe, knowing quite well that he could open such a safe in less than a minute.

Another moth fell to the floor under his light. He shook the drapery and three more fell out of it. Kneeling quickly, he counted seventeen moths upon the floor. *They were all dead.*

Wentworth stood up and drew in his breath thoughtfully. He turned to another piece of furniture and shook its covering. No moth fell to the floor. The covering of another piece of furniture, upon being shaken, rendered up one moth which flew away, very much alive.

Wentworth returned to the iron safe and regarded the seventeen dead moths upon the floor. What did the safe contain which caused the moths to die? The chemical odor, which escaped from it, was very slight indeed. But it showed that the door of the old fashioned safe did not fit perfectly. The very slight smell, which escaped, had killed the moths. What would happen to the man who *opened the door* of that safe?

What murderous weapon did the safe contain? And still more important, what thing of value did such a murderous weapon defend?

Wentworth knelt upon the floor with an ear against the safe door while his long fingers gently turned the knob. His eyes watched the door of the library as well as possible in the very subdued light. He listened intently, trying to hear the slight sound of the tumblers and also any other sound which might occur in the house. Few men would have knelt in such a way amid the shadows of a boarded up house and tampered with a great iron box which seemed to contain death.

But Wentworth did not open the safe. He rose to his feet and placed a hand against his forehead. Already he was being assailed by a slight headache. What chance would he have if he opened the door of that safe? As a matter of fact he had only been testing the combination. And he knew now, beyond question of doubt, that he could open the safe within a very few seconds.

Faintly, apparently from downstairs, there came the sound of a door opening and closing. Wentworth, listening at the library door, heard the unmistakable sound of steps upon the stairs. They were heavy steps and he noted that same apparent lameness which the unknown man had displayed in passing him upon his way out of the house. Was this man then the author of the murderous thing in the library?

Wentworth had replaced the drapery over the iron safe. Now he crossed the hall and stood silently in the doorway of the nearest unused bedroom while the man from below, with an occasional flash from an electric torch, steadily mounted the broad stairs.

It would seem as though two very dangerous men were alone together in the dark house.

CHAPTER 15
THE SPIDER FIGHTS DEATH

A T THE top of the stairs the man, who seemed to be carrying something, turned away from the entrance to the bedroom where Wentworth stood and entered the library, through the open doorway of which the soft glow of an electric lamp suddenly shone. Immediately Wentworth advanced toward the library door, placing his feet so delicately upon the floor that no sound warned of his approach. Carefully he peered into the library, his hand upon the pistol in his pocket.

The strange man was seated with his back to the door, and Wentworth stood watching, ready to step aside into the shadows at any moment. There came to him the familiar sound of a telephone being dialed, and Wentworth knew that the man had a telephone in his lap, although he could not see it.

While he waited for the connection to be made, Wentworth observed what the man had carried upstairs. A large Gladstone bag lay open before the iron safe, from which the drapery had been thrown back. The bag lay upon the floor in such a way that he could look into it, and he saw that it was quite empty. When a man brings a bag to a safe, he brings it for the purpose of putting something into the safe or for the purpose of taking something out of the safe. Since the Gladstone bag was empty Wentworth felt certain that the man was about to remove something.

But how could a man open the door of a safe from which a deadly gas exuded slightly even when that door was closed?

The gigantic crime was revealed to Wentworth as he lay in the hall.

The answer was simple and in plain view. A gas mask lay upon the floor beside the bag. Wentworth frowned. He wanted to open that safe himself.

Presently the strange man was speaking over the telephone in a low voice. "This is Dr. Quornelle," the man said. Then his voice dropped so low that Wentworth could not distinguish the words. Listening very intently, he could only gather the impression that the conversation was not to the satisfaction of the doctor. The indistinguishable words seemed to carry irritation and even suppressed anger.

In the dark hall Wentworth silently stretched himself upon the floor close to the wall by the library door and advanced his head so that he could see into the room and hear as much as possible. He was in such a position that he could withdraw his head instantly; and a head close to the floor was less apt to be detected than if it were at the height of a man.

He struggled to recognize the voice and almost thought that he did so, but could not be sure. The fact that the man was Dr. Quornelle did not prove that he was the great criminal.

Then, unexpectedly, Dr. Quornelle raised his voice at the telephone, and Wentworth heard his own name. He heard more, so much more that all doubt was swept from his mind.

"Blunton is dead," Dr. Quornelle said over the telephone, his voice raised in anger. "He was killed by Richard Wentworth who covered his tracks by using the 'Spider' seal. Nobody else could have done it."

At last Wentworth knew that he was close to the man he wanted. His hand felt the pistol in his pocket, but he hesitated to attack. To do so now might make it impossible to prove the innocence of Dorothy Canfield's sweetheart. It was necessary for him to learn much more before he struck.

"If Wentworth discovered Blunton's real mission, he may try to block us." Dr. Quornelle was speaking again. "Have steam up on the *Molly Ann* tonight at ten o'clock. We will have to go ahead without Blunton's diagram of the ship's strong room. We will meet the ship with the foreign debt payment two days out to sea, lie across her bow to windward and snuff out everybody on board with our gas. With the gold bars in our hold, we need never again bother about such little things as pay-rolls, diamonds or stocks and bonds. This is my great venture and it *must* succeed."

The gigantic crime was revealed to Wentworth as he lay in the hall. It was nothing less than the stealing of a huge foreign-debt payment that was on the ocean on its way to America. In the pitiless heart of the doctor was the calm intention to murder everyone on the great ship by the use of lethal gas… It was human brutality almost beyond belief.

AGAIN WENTWORTH felt the pistol in his pocket, and again he resisted the urge to kill such a man without delay. It would be a grand climax to fight this murderous criminal aboard his own ship on the eve of the colossal crime. And, in the meantime, he had other things to do. Wentworth's hand came away from the pistol in his pocket.

Dr. Quornelle replaced the receiver impatiently and set the instrument on the table by his side. With his back to Wentworth, lying by the door, he seemed to be gazing at the iron safe. Abruptly, as if the telephone conversation had altered his plans, he reached to the floor and picked up the gas mask, placing it in the drawer of a table upon the other side of his chair. Then he leaned forward and pulled the drapery back over the safe.

Not once had he turned so that his face could be seen from the doorway, and the high back of his chair even concealed his head. Undoubtedly he had decided against the immediate opening of the safe.

Wentworth waited patiently, watching, listening intently. The gloomy house, with its boarded up windows, seemed life-lessly silent. The high back of the chair in the library complete-ly concealed the man in that chair from Wentworth's view. He almost had the feeling that Dr. Quornelle was no longer there, but the fragrance of the Havana continued and some of the cigar smoke drifted under the shade of the small lamp which stood upon the table. And into that smoke by the lamp a hand rose presently from the chair, touched the dangling chain of the lamp, pulled it. The room was plunged into darkness.

For half an hour then there was silence. The fragrance of the cigar died down. The man in the library did not move.

Suddenly the silence was broken by a short burst of laughter. It was cruel laughter, almost insane, and it concluded as abrupt-ly as it had commenced. Dr. Quornelle had risen from his chair. Wentworth heard him coming toward the doorway and drew back his head just in time to escape a stab of light from a flash in the hand of the advancing man.

Dr. Quornelle came into the hall, his foot within an inch of Wentworth's head as he passed through the library doorway. He stood by the banister of the stairs and shot a beam from his flashlight down into the hall below. Still Wentworth was unable to obtain a view of the man's face.

After the single flash of light into the hall below, Dr. Quornelle stood still in the darkness. Apparently he was thinking and, if so, the result of his thought was not very pleasant. Again came a burst of hideous laughter, laughter which might find its cause in pain or death, sadist laughter perhaps.

The figure, which Wentworth could just distinguish in the darkness, moved away from the banister and became indistinguishable. Presently there was the sound of a key in a lock, and Wentworth knew that Dr. Quornelle was entering the locked room at the rear of the house. He heard the door open and close, and again he heard the sound of the key in the lock.

VERY CAUTIOUSLY Wentworth groped his way to the locked door. He placed his eye to the keyhole and saw daylight dimly, but could not discern any objects except what appeared to be a row of bottles upon a bench or long table.

Kneeling upon the floor, Wentworth turned his head sidewise and placed an ear flat against a panel of the door. He could hear the doctor moving around and suddenly he was surprised to hear him talking. Was it possible that someone, a prisoner perhaps was in that locked room with the doctor?

Wentworth listened intently, but could hear no answering voice when the doctor ceased speaking. He seemed to be talking to himself or to a person who refused to reply. Through the door it was impossible to understand what was being said, but the tone of voice carried cruelty and hatred.

The doctor stopped talking and presently Wentworth heard

him grunt as if he were exerting himself physically. Through the keyhole Wentworth caught a glimpse of his bent back. He seemed to be lifting some heavy object. There was the distinct thud of the object being set down after being lifted.

There came then another burst of the horrid laughter, and the key rattled unexpectedly in the lock. Wentworth just had time to regain the cover of the bedroom doorway.

Dr. Quornelle emerged from the locked room, slammed the door behind him and locked it again. He seemed very much excited, throwing the beam from his flashlight erratically around the hall and chuckling horridly to himself. Again he came very close to Wentworth, and suddenly halted as if he sensed something, perhaps another presence. Wentworth held his breath, but the doctor moved on and began to descend the stairs. His chuckling ceased and he began to go quietly, stealthily. Behind him Wentworth followed cautiously and as closely as he dared.

Dr. Quornelle reached the main floor and descended to the basement. Wentworth, following with expert stealth, saw him make his exit by means of the rear door which opened on the back yard. Not once had he been able to obtain a view of the doctor's face.

As soon as he dared he opened the back door gently and peered out. The yard was empty, the doctor, evidently, having crossed quickly to the door in the wall and passed out.

Wentworth retraced his steps to the second floor, his memory serving him so well that he did not need the aid of his flashlight. There were two things which aroused his interest, the iron safe and the locked room at the rear of the house. Each would seem to contain a secret to be discovered.

The situation appealed to his fancy in the extreme, and he was thoroughly enjoying himself. He decided to investigate the locked room first, since opening the safe, if the gas were as deadly as he anticipated, might render further work in the house uncomfortable if not actually dangerous.

The locked door gave him little trouble. He opened it almost as quickly as Dr. Quornelle had done with the regular key. There was considerable daylight in the room due to the fact that a board had been wrenched off the boarding of a window. What Wentworth saw was a small laboratory. There were the usual shelves of bottles, sinks, racks of test tubes, retorts and scales for analysis. Against the wall on one side of the room was a long fume chamber, a glass compartment for the carrying out of chemical experiments or operations which gave off obnoxious gasses. Such chambers are fairly air tight except that they have ducts for the entrance of air at the bottom when a fan is used to draw off the fumes through a vent at the top.

Wentworth swept the laboratory with his eyes, then sprang quickly to the fume chamber. Inside the long, box-like structure was a man.

He was lying on his back, bound and gagged, and one glance was sufficient to inform him that he had found Jack Selwyn. Notwithstanding the gag, Wentworth recognized the face as that of the photograph upon the back of which little Dorothy Canfield had so unwisely written the new name and address of her sweetheart.

SWIFTLY WENTWORTH threw up the long, sliding front of the fume chamber, then staggered back. Gas flowed out upon him, illuminating gas from a number of Bunsen burners inside the chamber. The fiendish method of death was apparent. It was apparent, too, that Selwyn was the object which Dr. Quornelle had struggled to lift and that the one-sided conversation had been due to the gag in Selwyn's mouth.

With unbelievable cruelty the doctor had probably taunted his victim while he lifted him into the fume chamber. He had then turned on the gas, closed the contraption and callously left the house chuckling with glee. Such a cruel and unnecessary form of death could only be the result of a diseased mind.

Cursing himself for not having investigated the locked room when he first entered the house, Wentworth held his breath while he leaned into the fume chamber and lifted Selwyn in his arms. He carried him across the room and deposited him upon the floor under the window from which part of the boarding had been removed. Rapidly he returned to the fume chamber and closed its sliding front, stopping the escape of further gas into the room. Then he knelt by the insensible man, swiftly cutting the bindings and removing the gag.

Jack Selwyn was a large and powerful man, but there was no strength left in his body. His chest was motionless, giving no sign of breathing. Wentworth pressed a wrist with his fingers, feeling for the pulse. There was no pulse.

Richard Wentworth had an attractive face. But, as he sat beside the man on the floor, that face contorted with so much anger that it became almost frightful. Here was the one thing which was unbearable to him—defeat! He had set out to bring happiness to a young couple he did not even know, a boy and girl in great trouble. The excitement and the danger enthralled him, but deep in his heart, unspoken to his friends, was the urge to bring happiness, romance, to others. And now, beside him, lay heartbreak for little Dorothy.

Abruptly the anger left his face and in its place came grim determination. He refused to accept defeat even when a heart had stopped beating.

Rapidly he removed Selwyn's coat and vest and turned the limp body upon its face, pulling one arm directly forward and bending the other at the elbow so that the cheek rested on the back of the hand, mouth toward the finger tips.* Then he knelt, straddling one of Selwyn's legs at the thigh.

For an instant Wentworth hesitated, then sent a fist crashing through the window to admit more air. He placed his hands on each side of Selwyn's back, just above the belt line, with his wrists four inches apart, thumb and fingers together; the little fingers over and following the line of the lowest rib; the tips of the fingers just out of his sight. For a second he swung the weight of his body forward until his shoulders were directly over his hands. Then he snapped his hands sidewise off his patient and swung his relaxed body to a resting position on his heels for a couple of seconds.

* EDITOR'S NOTE: We have asked the author to give this description in full. If all our readers memorized it, many additional lives would be saved.

Over and over again he repeated this operation, twelve to fifteen times per minute, forcing some air into and out of the lungs each time. He worked steadily, grimly. Minute followed minute, and half an hour passed. Still there was no sign of life. He continued the operation with the endurance of a great gymnast, knowing that it must be continued without a break for four hours or more before all hope was gone. His right hand, bleeding from the broken glass of the window, left Selwyn's shirt bloody. But Wentworth paid no attention to his own wound.

Each time that Wentworth relaxed, sitting upon his heels for two seconds, his head came on a level with the window so that he could see into the back yard below. Almost directly below him, so that he could just catch a glimpse of it each time he sat upright upon his heels, was the door in the wall which surrounded the yard. Automatically he watched that door as he worked, counting the seconds to maintain the regularity of the life-restoring operation.

An hour passed, and the muscles of the working man were tense with fatigue. There was no one to relieve him. To stop the operation was to rob young Selwyn of the slight chance which he might have to live and, also, to rob Wentworth, himself, of the slight chance of turning his seeming defeat into victory. He worked on, paying no attention to his wounded hand which was now encrusted with blood.

Then, suddenly, as he sat upright upon his heels, tired and aching, the door in the wall opened. A man came through and strode toward the house. He was visible to Wentworth only for a few seconds and, seen from almost directly above, his face was hidden by the brim of his hat. But the man walked with a very slight limp, and Wentworth knew that Dr. Quornelle was returning to the house.

Not for a second did Wentworth relax his efforts, not even when he jerked his pistol out of his pocket and dropped it beside him upon the floor. Nor would he break the rhythm of his operation at any cost. He would shoot it out with his enemy while he worked, freeing one hand perhaps for an instant's use of the pistol.

CHAPTER 16
A LIFE IN THE BALANCE

I T WOULD have been a nervous situation for most men. Wentworth was tense and alert as he worked over the insensible man, and he was very, very tired. But he was *not* nervous. It was not in his character to be nervous. Probably some day he would face the approach of his own death with nerves that left him the benefit of calm thought.

More minutes passed, fifteen of them, and nothing further happened. Silence dwelt in the house of the boarded windows. Even the street noises were cut off from the little laboratory at the back of the house. Then Wentworth felt the slightest of quivers in the body of Selwyn. He continued his efforts without pause and felt a very gentle, but natural breath. He reached for the pulse and could detect a faint heart beat. Still he continued to work. He knew that it was like cranking a car when the self starter fails. Sometimes the engine turns over a few times and stops again.

Soon the breathing became more certain, the heart beat more distinct. At last he stopped his work and selected a clean beaker from a laboratory table. Into it he poured some brandy from his flask and diluted it with water from a faucet. He lifted Selwyn's head and poured a little of the weak stimulant into his mouth. In ten minutes Selwyn, his head resting on his folded coat, was able to talk in a weak voice. Naturally he was bewildered. He had, he said, been dreaming, having a horrible nightmare.

Wentworth soothed him as if he were a small child, and gradually Selwyn's mind cleared. Out of a condition very similar to death, if not actually death itself, he had come back to the so-called realities of life, and his vigorous body began to pick up its old strength more rapidly than might have been expected.

His first words were for Dorothy. "Where is Dot?" he asked. "Is she all right?"

"She is safe and sound," Wentworth assured him.

"Oh! Then I guess everything will come out O.K."

Wentworth explained a little of the situation, refraining, at first, from putting searching questions, although he was very much puzzled as to why anybody should wish to kill this young man.

"Yes, I knew about you, Mr. Wentworth," Selwyn said. "Dot told me that she was going to ask you to help us."

Very slowly and gently Wentworth drew some of his story

from him. Selwyn had been awakened before dawn by a man who claimed to be a doctor and who said that Dorothy had been hurt in an accident and was calling for him. He was so upset and frightened about Dorothy that he gave scant thought to the strangeness at entering the doctor's house through a back yard.

Once inside the house, the doctor, a pistol in one hand and a flashlight in the other, had conducted him upstairs to the laboratory and there bound and gagged him.

"But where did the blood on your sheets come from?" Wentworth asked.

Selwyn smiled weakly. "When the doctor wakened me, I thought he was a policeman—and I hit him on the nose before he had time to explain who he was."

"And I thought it was your own life's blood," commented Wentworth dryly.

"I lay here for hours," Selwyn continued, "and then he put me in that horrible glass box."

The exertion of talking or the memory of the frightful moments of suffocation, before consciousness lapsed, turned the young man weak and faint. He became violently ill.

Wentworth gently held his head. Always his hand hovered near the pistol upon the floor, while his eyes darted continuously to the door. At any moment death might stalk through that door, and he had to be ready for instant action.

"But why did he want to kill me?" Selwyn asked faintly as his stomach settled and he felt a little better.

Wentworth looked closely at him. "Do you mean to tell me that you do not know?" he asked.

Selwyn shook his head.

"Do you know who took the diamonds away from you?"

Selwyn nodded. "Of course! It was my boss. Then he denied it and telephoned for the police, and I had to run. I had no chance."

"No," said Wentworth, "you are wrong. The man who took the diamonds from you is the man who just tried to murder you."

Selwyn looked his unbelief. He shook his head. "Couldn't be!" he protested. "He doesn't look like my old boss."

"He was made up to look like your employer." Wentworth insisted. "Remember that the light in the hall was not very bright when you met the man you thought was your employer and gave him the package of diamonds at his request. The interview was short and unexpected. You had no thought of treachery."

"But why does he want to kill me?"

"Obviously," replied Wentworth gravely, "you have no possession which he desires. Therefore, also obviously, you know something which he wishes to silence forever by death."

"But I don't know any such thing."

"A man may know many things," replied Wentworth, smiling, "which he does not know he knows."

A door slammed in the house—the first break in the silence. Softly Wentworth went to the door and placed his ear against it, but he could hear nothing. He dared not leave the still-weak

Selwyn there upon the floor, yet he wanted nothing better than to dart from the room, to merge himself into the shadows of the gloomy house and to fight the man who was below.

SLOWLY HE returned to the man whose life he had just saved and began to question him minutely about the brief interview he had had with his supposed employer.

"Don't you know," Wentworth said, "that you might have remained and proved your innocence? The diamonds could not have been found in your possession, and it would have been unbelievable that you should have returned to your employer and invented such an apparently absurd story if it were not true."

"I know," admitted Selwyn gloomily, "but I lost my presence of mind and ran away. Nobody would believe me innocent after I ran away." He paused. "There is one little thing that happened when I gave the package of diamonds to my boss."

"What is that?" Wentworth shot at him.

"The little finger of his left hand was off at the big knuckle," Selwyn answered. "Of course I was not intimate with him, and I had never noticed it before. It sort of fascinated me, and I guess I didn't look very closely at his face. He saw me staring at his hand and he jerked it away, kind of mad."

"And that tells the story," said Wentworth decisively. "He was afraid that some day you would be caught and give evidence regarding the missing end of his finger. Your death would make that impossible."

Gradually little things were piecing themselves together. Wentworth remembered the glove on the left hand of Mr. X in the Penthouse of Madame Pompé. He remembered the big marquise ring, covering the joint of the little finger of the drunken man at the rooming house of Dorothy Canfield. No doubt the ring aided in concealing the junction of an artificial finger.

The great criminal was the man who had defrauded the diamond merchant by deceiving his innocent clerk. He was the drunken man, lying upon the bed and snoring with his face to the wall. He was Mr. X with the two guns in Madame Pompé's penthouse. The great criminal was Dr. Quornelle, who was a trifle lame because his thigh had been pierced by Wentworth's rapier in Dorothy Canfield's room.

Wentworth gave Selwyn a few more sips of brandy and water. The man really should have been in bed with a nurse giving him a spoonful of soup every now and then, but he had a very sturdy frame and appeared as though he might soon be able to walk.

Wentworth replaced his flask and turned swiftly to the door, pistol in hand. More sound could be heard from the house outside that door. There were heavy footsteps ascending the stairs. They came irregularly, not lame, but unsteady.

Through the keyhole Wentworth caught glimpses of a flash-light. He hesitated to open the door even a trifle, since the daylight in the room would filter through and reveal the fact that the door was no longer closed and locked as Dr. Quornelle had left it.

The unsteady footsteps came to the head of the stairs and

stopped. Then they moved forward, but Wentworth could not tell toward which room they were headed.

Suddenly a man began speaking in a voice a bit too loud to be natural. He spoke slowly and enunciated his words with a slight difficulty. The man was drunk.

"Dr. Quornelle," the voice commenced impressively, "you are saluted by the New York press in general and by *The Evening Standard* in particular."

The answer, if any, could not be heard, the door cutting it off from Wentworth. But Wentworth recognized the loud voice and knew that Sparks, the reporter, was in the house and still rather drunk. How he came to be in the house was a mystery. Handicapped by the weak condition of Selwyn, Wentworth hesitated to open the door, something he was to regret.

"What I want to know, Dr. Quornelle," the loud voice of Sparks continued slowly and solemnly, "is who, where, when, why and—and what for?"

Again there was a brief silence, and once more the loud voice of Sparks boomed forth.

"My dear Dr. Quornelle. I 'pologize. I thought I stated question most explish—most ex—very clearly. I shall repeat. In interest of people of New York, I wish to know why you took Madame Pompé away from big, fat radio announcer."

There may have been words in reply and there may not have been. Wentworth could not hear any, but he heard another kind of reply. A pistol shot shattered the silence of the house, and there followed the thud of a falling body.

Desperately Wentworth threw open the laboratory door and

flung himself into the hall, low down upon his knees, his pistol held forward in one hand.

Electric light streamed from the library door, and through it a man leaped into the outer darkness of the hall, firing through the open laboratory door with a decision which was taken instantaneously in the very act of leaping.

Wentworth had no opportunity of using his pistol, not knowing whether the leaping man were friend or foe until after the second shot had been fired.

The house was intensely silent after the two pistol shots. The fleeing man had vanished into the deep darkness. Wentworth crouched low down against a wall where the subdued daylight from the laboratory did not reach him. Behind him, in the laboratory, a strong young man lay weak and ill from the close approach of death.

What lay in the library, where the electric light shone, could not be seen—but it was very, very still.

CHAPTER 17
SPARKS' LAST STORY

THE PROBLEM that confronted Wentworth was a difficult one. Behind him, upon the floor of the laboratory, lay a fine young fellow unable to defend himself and whose life had been attempted once and would be attempted again if the opportunity occurred. In the library across the hall was the reporter, Sparks, a likable chap who had drunkenly barged into dynamite and who was undoubtedly shot, perhaps fatally.

At large in the great, black house was a devil.

Of course Wentworth could call the police—if he could reach the telephone in the library. But even to do that, he would have to leave Selwyn too far behind for the safety of that young man. To carry or support the sick man into the library would be to expose him to a bullet in passing through the lighted doorway.

The telephone for the moment was out of the question and, in any case, Wentworth did not want the police. He liked to fight his own battles, sometimes in ways that the police could not tolerate.

Wentworth made up his mind. Darkness and secrecy were no longer of value. He felt his way to the head of the stairs, found the electric wall switch and flooded the hall with light. The light showed no one in the hall, but there were doors through which his enemy might appear at any moment. He passed quickly from door to door, reaching for the key on the inside and locking the door on the outside. Then he returned to the laboratory and found Selwyn leaning unsteadily in the doorway. Together they walked slowly to the library.

"Sit here and watch the stairs," said Wentworth, directing Selwyn to take a chair at the entrance of the library…

At first Wentworth thought Sparks was dead. The reporter was lying upon the floor beside the Gladstone bag in front of the draped safe. But the wounded man moved his head a trifle to look up, and in his eyes was sudden pleasure at sight of Wentworth. He tried to smile.

Wentworth knelt beside the wounded reporter, and unbuttoned his vest and felt the warm blood surging through the front of his shirt. Richard Wentworth knew wounds and he realized that Sparks would never interview anyone again, drunk or sober. He crumpled the shirt and pressed it against the wound in the chest to stop the flow of blood as much as possible. But he knew it was useless.

"Glad to see me?" asked Sparks in a weak voice, much sobered by the shock of his wound.

"It's bully!" Wentworth's voice was warm.

There were a few moments of silence while Wentworth supported the reporter's head with his left arm.

"I think I'll telephone for an ambulance and get you patched up," Wentworth said at last.

"It's no use, Mr. Wentworth," Sparks replied. "I'm going. It was pretty hard sledding before you came in, but it's kind of easy going with you beside me."

"Nonsense!" protested Wentworth. "We'll patch you up and run down many a good story together in days to come."

"You do something for me?"

"I certainly shall."

"What time is it?"

Wentworth glanced at his wrist watch. "It's ten o'clock."

"Will you dial my newspaper and give me the telephone?" The voice was becoming a little weaker. "I got a job to do."

WENTWORTH DID as he was requested, reaching up to the table for the telephone. When he had dialed he held the telephone so that the reporter could speak into it.

"This is Sparks," he said, trying to increase the strength of his voice. "Give me the city desk and make it snappy... Hello!

City desk?… This is Sparks. I've got a hot story and it's exclusive. It's short. Ready?… A reporter named Sparks of *The Evening Standard* was murdered this morning by Dr. Sylvester Quornelle. During an interview Dr. Quornelle, without any warning, shot the reporter through the chest. The reporter died a few minutes after ten. That's all. Do I get a by line?… I'm drunk and I'm fired? I guess you're right, Mr. City Editor. I'm fired all right. Perhaps I'll get a by line in the next town."

The voice, very weak, trailed to an end, and Sparks' head rolled sideways upon Wentworth's supporting arm.

Wentworth lifted the telephone to his own ear. "This is Richard Wentworth," he barked. "The story you just heard was authentic. Your reporter has this minute died in my arms. He did the most courageous piece of reporting that I ever heard of. If you don't give him a by line, I'll see to it personally that you lose your job and are run out of journalism!"

Wentworth replaced the receiver abruptly and lowered Sparks' head gently to the floor. He looked at freshly bloodied hand for a moment, then turned to Jack Selwyn who sat by the library door very much shocked.

"By God, Selwyn," he said, "that's the way to die!" Wentworth stepped over the body of Sparks and threw the drapery back from the iron safe.

"Now then, Selwyn," he said, "I must work quickly. The newspaper will report the murder of Sparks to the police and they will be here in a very few minutes. We must be gone before they arrive. Move out into the hall a little and watch the stairs carefully."

Before he had quite finished speaking, he had pressed an ear against the safe and his expert fingers had commenced to manipulate the dial of the combination. A minute passed and he seemed satisfied. From the table drawer, where Dr. Quornelle had placed it, he took the gas mask and donned it. Turning back to the safe, a single tug on the handle swung the heavy door open.

The first object which met Wentworth's gaze brought him great satisfaction. Standing in a large open compartment of the big safe was the old Ming vase of reticulated porcelain which had been stolen from his apartment. Wentworth could not refrain from feeling the smooth surface of its aubergine enamel with his finger tips. He removed it lovingly from the safe and placed it upon the floor beside him. Then he searched pigeon-holes and drawers with great rapidity.

There were many securities, bonds and stock certificates, and there were some packages of high-denomination bills. These he returned to their receptacles but, in a small drawer, he found something which interested him very much, a package of glittering diamonds. In all probability they were the diamonds which Jack Selwyn was accused of stealing. He dropped them quickly into a pocket of his coat.

At the bottom of the safe was a dish containing what was probably an acid and which was very likely the means of creating the deadly poison gas after the safe was last closed. Wentworth had no time to examine it closely. He hurriedly changed the combination of the safe, then closed and locked the door. If Dr. Quornelle should attempt to open his safe before the arrival of the police, he would find considerable difficulty in doing so.

Wrapping the Chinese vase in the drapery from the safe, Wentworth tucked it under his arm and joined Jack Selwyn in the hall.

"Strong enough to negotiate the stairs?" Wentworth asked.

"Yes," Selwyn replied with assurance. "I am even beginning to feel a little bit hungry."

"Good man! Keep a lookout behind while I go ahead. This fiend may still be in the house. It's impossible to be sure of anything about him. That's what makes him interesting."

SLOWLY THEY descended the stairs to the main floor. There was no person in sight, and the house was quite silent. Wentworth found the electric switch and flooded the hall of the main floor with light, watching keenly for any sudden attack from one of the surrounding doorways. Nothing happened.

They passed through the hall and descended slowly to the basement, and again Wentworth switched on the electric light. Still there was no sign of anybody, and silence surrounded them. Wentworth unlocked the door for tradespeople, through which he entered the house, and they passed out into daylight.

The basement of Dr. Quornelle's house was below the level of the street, and stone steps led up to the sidewalk from the tradesman's entrance. Seated upon the top step was an old man who appeared to be resting while he smoked a pipe with bowed head. Beside him was a broom with which he had evidently been sweeping the steps. He wore neither coat nor vest and his long brown neck protruded from a shirt unadorned by a collar.

The old man showed no surprise at the sight of two men issuing from the door below him.

On the sidewalk, while they waited for a taxi, Wentworth stood directly behind the old man who continued to sit very still where he smoked with bowed head.

"Do you work here, my man?" asked Wentworth. "No speeka da Eenglish," the old man answered in a quavering voice without turning around.

Wentworth placed the drapery-wrapped vase carefully on the sidewalk and addressed the old man in Italian, while he extracted a cigarette from his case.

The old man answered in Greek, which Wentworth recognized but could not understand.

"I guess the police will be too late to catch the murderer," Jack Selwyn remarked, leaning back wearily in the taxi as they drove away. He had gone through a tremendous ordeal, and he was far from strong.

"Perhaps," was the dubious reply.

"You think the criminal is still there?"

"Maybe." Again the reply was dubious, but suddenly Wentworth snapped into life. "Drive back to the house, where you picked us up," he sharply addressed the taxi driver.

The taxi turned abruptly and returned to the house with the boarded windows. Wentworth sprang to the sidewalk and looked down the steps to the servants' entrance. The old man had disappeared. Chagrined, he returned to the taxi and they drove away once more, just as a radio police car swooped around a corner, passed them and drew up at the house which they had left.

"Why did you look for the old man again?" asked Selwyn.

"Because the old man was Dr. Sylvester Quornelle."

"Are you sure?" Selwyn was amazed.

"Quite!" returned Wentworth. "He was the same height and weight as Dr. Quornelle. He kept his left hand in his right pocket as he sat on the steps, and Dr. Quornelle has some difficulty in concealing the identifying defect in the little finger of his left hand. The old man on the steps kept his left leg straight out before him as if it were a bit stiff, and Dr. Quornelle's left leg is a trifle lame, probably because of a puncture I gave it with a rapier. There is no doubt about the identity of the old man on the steps."

From the sidewalk a newsboy shouted an extra.

"Ship docks with Spider on board. All passengers detained for search."

CHAPTER 18
THE DOCTOR RETURNS

WENTWORTH, ARRIVED in his apartment, took Selwyn directly to the music room and made him lie down upon a lounge and rest. The young man was still weak and faint, and only an excellent constitution had permitted him to bear up as he had done after what he had gone through.

"A cup of hot bouillon, Jenkyns," Wentworth directed the

butler, "and ask Miss Canfield if she will be kind enough to come here."

And a little later this strange man, who fought and sometimes killed without a qualm, sat upon the organ bench with his back to the young couple on the lounge. The blinds were drawn and a soft, rosy light flooded the room from concealed lamps, low, gentle music came from the pipes of the organ, music that could enter a young girl's heart. Sometimes Wentworth used the rheostat, under the keyboard, to alter the lighting so that it suited the mood of the music he was playing. He did not speak at all and there was very little conversation upon the lounge where Dorothy sat beside her Jack and occasionally held a spoonful of bouillon to his lips.

It was such a moment as this which gave to Wentworth that peculiar satisfaction which rivaled the thrill he experienced in moments of violent combat and great danger. There were two opposing sides to his character and probably neither side could exist without the other.

"He is wonderful," whispered Dorothy. "I wish I could sit here for ever and ever—with you, Jack."

And that was just the feeling that Richard Wentworth intended Dorothy to feel.

But there were other things for Wentworth to do. His friend the inspector had much to talk about in the library. A report of Sparks' murder had been telephoned from Police Headquarters.

"Were you in Dr. Quornelle's house?" the inspector wanted to know. "What were you doing there, Mr. Wentworth?"

"Why the devil did you turn that young reporter loose?" Wentworth countered. "You sent him to his death."

"The charge against him wasn't serious, Mr. Wentworth, and he seemed to be a friend of yours. By the way, here's your rapier stick. It's a beauty, but it's against the law."

Wentworth smiled and tossed the stick to Ram Singh who was passing at the moment. "The law is sometimes a dangerous enemy to freedom," he remarked. "Have you picked up Dr. Quornelle yet?"

"Not yet. An old caretaker, sweeping up in front of the house, said that he had been employed there for about a year but had never seen Dr. Quornelle. The house has been closed for a long time, you know."

"I should advise you to check up on that old caretaker," said Wentworth. "But I shall wager that you never find him again."

"Why do you say that?"

"Because the old caretaker was Dr. Quornelle."

The inspector looked hard at Wentworth, saw that he was in earnest and dashed for a telephone.

NITA VAN SLOAN sent word to Wentworth suggesting that he join her for breakfast. He found her in the dining room busy with a grapefruit.

"Dick, what is this all about? I feel that there is some big thing, back of it all, that none of us knows anything about. Am I right?"

"Yes." Wentworth was quietly emphatic. "There is something very big behind it all. Very soon an attempt will be made to perpetrate one of the greatest crimes which history could record.

I now know the name of the criminal, and I know what he is going to try to do although I do not yet know how he hopes to do it. In just a little while I shall be able to explain everything to you. In the meantime there maybe another woman—a bit off color. Do you mind?"

Nita tried to keep a stiff upper lip in the face of impending danger. "Not if she is interesting," he said. "A lot of women in this world are a bit off color, Dick."

"But this one is a bad egg."

"So? Well, if she is necessary, I'll put up with her." From the doorway Ram Singh was beckoning, and Wentworth left the dining room quickly. He found Professor Brownlee in the library. The old man's eyes were gleaming with excitement.

"I've got it!" the professor exclaimed, then dropped his voice very low as they sat close together. "It's a beauty! The idea came to me like a flash. All the best ideas come that way."

"Good!" Wentworth looked expectant. "What is it?"

From his pocket the professor took a cigarette lighter and placed it in Wentworth's hand. "You can't see the junction of the secret compartment," he explained. "It is covered with varnish which is the same color as the metal. One twist and it opens, but of course you have to break the coating of varnish to do it."

"Very clever, but is that all?" asked Wentworth.

"That is just the beginning," the professor replied enthusiastically. "The hidden cavity is air tight, the varnish having been put on in a vacuum. The design on the die is done on a thin film which entirely dissipates thirty seconds after the air strikes it."

"Excellent!" exclaimed Wentworth appreciatively, slipping the Lighter into his pocket.

Suddenly the pleasure died out of Professor Brownlee's face. He loved Dick Wentworth, the Dick of the old college days, and he feared that the younger man might not always succeed in the dangerous things he did.

"Ever think of getting married, Dick?" he asked rather wistfully. "There's a lot in that cottage and honeysuckle idea, you know. It might even work with a Park Avenue apartment and orchids—with the right girl."

Wentworth's face, too, was a little wistful. "Some day perhaps, Professor," he answered with a touch of sadness in his voice. "Some day, but—not yet!"

THEY WERE interrupted by Jenkyns. It was a telephone call. Wentworth took it on the telephone in the library which he reached from where he sat beside the professor.

"Hello!"

"This is Madame Pompé—Corinne."

Wentworth was very cordial and expressed himself as being delighted to hear her throaty, fascinating voice once more. He even used her first name with friendly intimacy.

"I'm in terrible trouble," she explained. "He beat me until I told him that I had promised to visit you tonight. Then he said that he would strangle me if I went near you."

Wentworth appropriately expressed his sorrow for her and

his anger toward the man who had abused her. He suggested that she inform the police and ask for their protection.

"Oh!" she moaned heartrendingly. "I can't! I can't! The police could never protect me. I'm terrified of him and I don't know what to do. Won't you help me, Mr. Wentworth? Won't you protect me—Dick?"

Wentworth winced at her use of his first name, but he felt nevertheless that she was probably in serious trouble—perhaps in real danger. Anybody connected with such a man as Dr. Quornelle must always be in danger.

"What do you suggest?" he asked. "I can't take you to Europe at the present time, you know."

"Please help me," she pleaded, her voice shaking. "I'll do anything you say. If you will only help me, I'll tell you his real name. I'll tell it to you now over the telephone."

"My dear lady," returned Wentworth, "I know his name, and he knows that I know it. His name is Dr. Sylvester Quornelle."

She did not reply, but just sobbed with that deep, seductive voice of hers which had made such a hit in radio singing.

He interrupted. "Listen, Corinne! Come over this evening as you promised and I'll see what I can do for you." After all, he felt that he might be somewhat to blame for her situation and he could hardly stand by and let her be murdered.

"I can't!" she exclaimed. "I would be dead before I reached you if I tried to come in the evening. My only chance is to come in the afternoon. Please save me and I'll do anything in the world for you—Dick."

Again he winced at the use of his first name, but his voice

seemed to express his pleasure. "All right, Corinne. Come over this afternoon if you can get away. And, by the way—"

"Yes?"

"Bring an overnight bag."

"An overnight bag?"

"Yes."

"Oh, Dick!"

Wentworth replaced the telephone upon the table.

"Now what the devil did she think I meant?" he grumbled as if he didn't know.

JACK SELWYN was put to bed. A long sleep was what he most needed to restore his strength. Nita and Dorothy were visiting in Nita's bedroom with Apollo as additional company. Stanley Kirkpatrick, Commissioner of Police of New York, lay very still upon his bed, but insisted upon talking briefly with the secretaries who came and went.

Wentworth was a little surprised to receive a request to visit the Commissioner and found the patient looking remarkably well. It seemed as though the doctors had been mistaken about the seriousness of his hurt, but they still maintained that it would be too great a risk to move him from the apartment for several days.

Commissioner Kirkpatrick was quite well enough to talk.

"Wentworth," he said rather sharply, "I have received a report of a killing on an old pier down at the foot of West 96th Street. The dead man has the seal of the Spider upon his forehead, and he was killed before the arrival of the ship which is supposed to be bringing the Spider to New York."

"Remarkable!" exclaimed Wentworth, lighting a cigarette from the lighter which had been given to him by Professor Brownlee. "I am so busy with this new case that I can't very well help you about the Spider just now." He held the lighter for a moment in his hand, looking at it speculatively.

"I see that you have a new lighter," said the Commissioner, frowning.

Wentworth looked inquiringly at Kirkpatrick. "Would you care to examine it?" he asked, extending the lighter toward the man on the bed.

"No thank you." The refusal was a bit crisp. "You would scarcely offer it to me if there were anything incriminating connected with it."

"On the contrary," replied Wentworth, smiling, "that is exactly what I *would* do in order to make you think exactly what you are thinking now."

The Commissioner remained silent. Undoubtedly he was again slightly suspicious of Wentworth. But it was plain that he had nothing further to say, and Wentworth withdrew.

MADAME POMPÉ arrived late in the afternoon and was shown to her room by the ever more and more surprised Jenkyns, who was not at all accustomed to working in homes which admitted so flamboyant a lady as the ex-radio-singer.

Wentworth had found Dorothy and told her about the arrival of Madame Pompé. "Treat her as if she had never twisted your arm," he said. "Just act as though you had never seen her before. Can you do it?"

Dorothy thought that she could act that way if Wentworth

wished it. She had such faith in the man that his wish was law to her.

It was just before dinner that the unusual party first assembled, for cocktails in the music room. Selwyn was still in bed, as was the Commissioner, but Nita and Dorothy were present, together with Wentworth and the inspector, to welcome Madame Pompé.

Madame Pompé seemed quite composed and carried herself very well indeed after a slight start upon beholding Dorothy Canfield. She did, however, seem a little uncomfortable physically, moving restlessly and bending forward so that she did not lean against the back of her chair.

"Is that chair not comfortable, Madame Pompé?" asked Wentworth. "May I get you another one?"

"It isn't the chair," she replied. "This gown is not cut very low behind, but you can pull it out some and look down if you want to know what the trouble is."

With this remarkable statement, she removed a light scarf from her shoulders and turned her back for inspection. Although the dress was not cut extremely low behind, it was quite low enough to present an amazing spectacle.

Wentworth glanced at her back and rose to his feet to avail himself of the permission for further inspection. He pulled out the dress as suggested and actually used his flashlight so that he could examine her back almost down to the waist. He beckoned to the inspector, who joined him and also peered down.

The sight of two men peering down a lady's back by means

inspector rushed from the dining room in the direction of the alarming sound, which seemed to have come from one of the bedrooms. He was followed by every policeman in the apartment, all of them clustering around the door of Madame Pompé's bedroom, from which smoke seemed to be issuing.

In the excitement Madame Pompé and Nita ran into the hall, but hesitated to go farther, leaving little Dorothy rather terrified in the dining room. Suddenly Madame Pompé twisted a pungent cloth around Nita's head, covering her mouth. Nita choked and half swooned as the more powerful woman opened the front door and dragged her into the hall.

The elevator, which came almost instantly when Madame Pompé rang, took them down without any stop, took them past the ground floor into the basement. Out through the service entrance Nita was dragged by Madame Pompé and the elevator man. Almost losing consciousness, she found herself in a taxi, seated between her two captors.

The elevator man unbuttoned his uniform, took off his cap and began to rub some makeup from his face.

"My dear Miss Van Sloan," he said, "please accept Dr. Quornelle's apology for the roughness of your removal. But please remember that you will be handled much more roughly if you make any resistance or attempt an outcry!"

CHAPTER 19
THE SPIDER STRIKES

RICHARD WENTWORTH was again upon his way to visit the *Molly Ann* at the foot of West 96th Street. This time he meant to penetrate to the very heart of that iniquitous ship and to come to grips, if possible, with the criminals who manned it. It was a dangerous undertaking—one which would have been undertaken by the police only in large numbers. Yet Wentworth took with him only Ram Singh, that devoted Oriental who had been with him upon so many adventures.

Ram Singh sat silently upon one of the little chairs before his master in the tonneau of the taxi. Although there was a bond of unselfish affection between them, the native would never think of sitting upon the same seat with his master unless some clever stratagem or serious necessity required it. Ram Singh lost none of his self-respect by looking upon the world and realizing that all men were not equal—and he increased his self-respect by the conviction that he served a master whom surpassed all men. Once when he had been wounded Wentworth had carried him in his arms like a baby while he rode a swaying camel for five hours over the Sindh Desert. There was no lack of sympathy between master and servant.

West 96th Street drops steeply toward the Hudson River and lights grow dimmer as Broadway is left behind. The street dips below a causeway which carries the famous Riverside Drive and emerges for a short block to end at the railroad tracks upon the other side of which the rickety piers are usually shrouded in darkness at night.

Wentworth dismissed the taxi at the tracks and walked slowly with Ram Singh into the darkness upon the other side. But on this night there were some lights to be seen amid the darkness, and those lights came from the *Molly Ann*. At the entrance to the pier they halted for a few minutes in the deep shadows.

The lights on the *Molly Ann* were dim, but that was to be expected from such an old tramp steamer. Yet they seemed dimmer and fewer than many an old tub might exhibit. From the single black funnel of the ship a dark plume of smoke was rising against the blue of the night sky. Undoubtedly steam was being raised in preparation for sailing.

But the few dim lights and the silence did not seem natural. A feeling of evil and of danger was about the place.

The two silent figures advanced slowly upon the pier. Through the darkness ahead of them there became visible a steeply inclined gangway which gave access to the ship from the low dock. Nobody seemed to be using the gangway, and the ship seemed dead except for the dim lights and the black smoke mounting from the funnel.

Slowly the two men continued to advance. They reached the gangway and Wentworth led the way up its steep ascent. Not a word had been spoken since they left the taxi. Neither knew what was going to happen, but they understood each other so well that words were scarcely necessary.

At the top of the gangway a man stepped out of some shadows and barred the way. He seemed to be the only man around, and in his hand he carried a marlinespike, which can become a very ugly weapon when wielded by a seafaring man.

Wentworth halted. "I would like to see the captain," he said.

"No visitors allowed!" the man answered in a surly manner, peering at the indolent stranger who had addressed him.

"What cargo are you carrying?" Wentworth questioned indifferently.

Instead of answering, the man raised the marlinespike to strike. But Wentworth shot a fist into his face with such suddenness and with such strength that the iron tool thumped upon the deck and the man went over backward. He struck his head upon a stanchion in his fall and lay quite still. Wentworth rubbed his knuckles and, followed closely by Ram Singh, stepped over the fallen man and ascended the companionway to the main deck.

THE DECK was not lighted, and it was almost necessary for them to feel their way forward. Darkness and silence surrounded them. Not a man was to be seen, but it was impossible to believe that the man with the marlinespike was the only one on board. At least there must be men in the engine room, where a dynamo gave life to the few dim lights which were to be seen.

Under the bridge Wentworth found the captain's cabin and peered inside. It was unlighted and empty. He looked down into the forward well where he had seen the rows of metal cylinders. The cylinders were no longer there, and he guessed that they had been stowed out of sight in the hold.

Only from the bridge, above them, did there seem to be any indication of life. A faint light shone down the companionway which led to that seat of control. Very cautiously Wentworth ascended the steps. Quite as cautiously and very closely Ram Singh followed him. So quietly did the two reach the bridge that a man, leaning against the starboard rail and looking down the river, did not hear them.

"Are you the captain?" Wentworth asked behind the man's back.

"Mate," the man answered, wheeling about in the dim light. "Who the hell are you?"

"Gas inspector," retorted Wentworth glibly. "The chief sent me aboard to test the cylinders."

The mate may have been a good navigator, but he was none too bright otherwise. His mouth opened in amazement. "Did Dr. Quornelle tell you what was in those cylinders?" he asked incredulously.

"Sure!" Wentworth laughed. "Poison gas."

"Are you one of us?" the mate demanded. "Do you get a cut of the big haul when we make it?"

Before Wentworth could reply, the mate caught sight of Ram Singh standing motionless at the head of the companionway. His suspicions aroused at last, he went into action much faster than he had been capable of thinking. From his pocket he jerked a pistol and fired at Wentworth as quickly as he raised it.

Wentworth, however, saw the pistol as it was raised and, in the dim light, ducked just before the shot. From his own pocket he drew forth something which produced a husky, coughing sound—and the mate slid silently to the deck of the bridge.

Once more the powerful air pistol had quietly done its work

and had ended the career of a man who had been willing to assist in the murdering of a thousand people on board a great liner.

Leisurely Wentworth knelt and took out his little cigarette lighter, the old lighter, which contained the seal that would make many impressions. Carefully and with great satisfaction he pressed the design of the spider upon the mate's forehead.

But the mate's pistol shot had been heard. The sound of heavy footsteps came from the deck below. The footsteps drew near and halted beneath the bridge. A man began to ascend the companionway. He halted half way and called up to the mate. Receiving no answer, there came the sound of voices in consultation, followed by a brief moment of silence.

Wentworth motioned to Ram Singh, and the two of them stepped into the empty chart house behind the bridge. Apparently it was to be a fight with the odds against them. They could only wait and, when the time came, think fast and shoot straight. Wentworth was sorry about the mate's pistol shot. His air-pistol was quiet. But ordinary shooting would soon call the police, which might add a great deal to the danger of the situation he faced.

AS THEY waited in the chart house, one of the men, unseen by Wentworth, raised his head above the deck of the bridge and caught a glimpse of the mate's body lying beside the wheel. There were whispered words and the scurrying of feet.

After a considerable pause a voice called from the deck below and was clearly heard through the open window of the chart house.

"Who are you up there?"

"Send the captain up," Wentworth called back.

"Captain's not aboard," the voice returned.

"Then come up yourself," Wentworth answered.

There was more silence and then: "Come down or we'll turn on some of the gas."

This was a contingency which Wentworth had not antici-pated. Even so, it gave him satisfaction because he now knew that the entire crew were aware of the murderous contents of the cylinders. It had not been his wish to injure innocent members of the frightful expedition which Dr. Quornelle was planning. All compunction left him upon hearing the threat to turn on some of the gas. They were all equally guilty of the intention to commit murder.

"If you turn on the gas, you will kill yourselves," he called back in answer to their threat.

There was a hoarse laugh and the voice replied: "We got gas masks."

"So have I," lied Wentworth without a moment of hesitation.

More silence followed and then, unexpectedly, a shot crashed through the floor of the chart house, fired from the captain's cabin directly beneath. Another bullet came through the chart house roof, fired from the crow's nest. Neither bullet did any harm, but more would follow. And, in the end one of them would find its intended mark. In the end, too, the shooting would probably be reported to the police by the watchman at the railroad crossing.

The man in the crow's nest proved easy to handle. Wentworth

stepped out upon the bridge and took careful aim before firing with his silent pistol. The man, who was leaning far out, slipped forward and fell to the deck with an ugly thump. There were no more shots through the roof of the chart house.

But more were being fired now through the flooring from the captain's cabin. It was becoming dangerous in the chart house and Wentworth called Ram Singh to join him on the bridge. As he did so, a police whistle sounded in the distance. In the end, of course, Wentworth wanted the police to come and take charge of the ship with its murderous cargo of poison gas, but he hoped to get away before they arrived.

The men on the deck below, however, had also heard the police whistle and ceased firing in consequence. They wished for the presence of the police—even less than did Wentworth. They could not, however, allow their antagonistic visitors to remain alive upon the bridge. Up from the engine room and out from the forecastle they came and assembled at the foot of the ladder leading to the bridge. They were desperate because they knew that failure of their enterprise would probably mean life imprisonment for them, if not death in the electric chair.

Wentworth and Ram Singh were also in a desperate situation. A police emergency car could now be heard, in the distance. They were between the police and the criminals whom they had sought to destroy.

"Ram Singh," said Wentworth, "can you dive off the bridge, swim under the ship and come up beneath the pier where you can hide?"

The Hindu nodded and was about to speak when there was

a violent scuffling of feet upon the companionway leading to the bridge. A concerted attack was being made. It came swiftly, savagely, and it was made by desperate men who had been toughened and coarsened in the free-for-alls of seafaring life. SUCH AN attack was not easily repulsed. Wentworth shot the first man who reached the bridge, and Ram Singh met the second man with his knife. But the third and fourth men sprang over the bodies of their comrades and were upon them.

Others followed. It became a terrific hand-to-hand conflict, Ram Singh fighting with his knife and Wentworth with a marlinespike which he wrenched from the hand of an assailant. Only the narrowness of the bridge saved them by preventing too many of their attackers from reaching them at the same time. As it was, they were forced back to the end of the bridge which overhung the pier.

Suddenly, amid the grunts and curses of the mêlée, what was literally a bellow burst upon the air.

"All hands off me bridge!" the words were roared.

The fighting seamen, some wounded, disengaged themselves, scrambled to the companionway and almost flung themselves to the deck below. Wentworth leaned back against the rail and found himself facing one of the largest men he had ever seen. The captain of the *Molly Ann* had come aboard his ship.

At first the captain thought that Wentworth was one of his fighting crew who had failed to obey his command. He sprang forward with a hand like a ham lifted to strike. But he saw his mistake and stopped his hand just as the emergency police car screamed its way out upon the old pier below them.

"Are you a policeman, a detective?" the captain growled. "Damn you!"

Without waiting for a reply the huge man rushed at Wentworth. It seemed as though the smaller man could have no chance at all. But, at the last moment, Wentworth bent suddenly down and slipped his head and shoulders between the big man's legs. Then his muscles tautened as he heaved upward, and the towering captain rose above the side rail of the bridge to be carried on by his own impetuous rush into a curving fall which ended in a crash upon the rotten planking far below on the old pier.

Flood lights shot from the emergency car of the police and began to play over the *Molly Ann.* It was only a matter of moments before the police would be swarming upon the ship, before they would round up its crew and begin a thorough investigation regarding the business and cargo of that ship… The *Molly Ann* would never carry out its great crime upon the high seas.

But Richard Wentworth might also have his career ended if he did not succeed in escaping both from the police and from the criminals with whom he had interfered. Swiftly he dragged Ram Singh to the other end of the bridge, the end which overhung the water.

"Jump!" he commanded.

Ram Singh hesitated, not liking to leave his master. Wentworth frowned, Ram Singh salaamed slowly in resignation, then sprang over the rail and struck the water in a perfect dive, leaving behind him only a short gurgle and some bubbles.

Richard Wentworth, alone upon the bridge of the *Molly Ann*, looked up at the dark blue of the sky and down at the three still forms upon the deck of the bridge at his feet. He shrugged his shoulders as if impressed by the futility of man in the midst of the universe.

There was a rush of policemen up the gangway from the pier. Shouts were heard and orders.

Methodically Wentworth pressed the seal of the Spider upon the forehead of the man who had headed the rush from the deck below. He looked at the man who had fought with Ram Singh and saw that there was a little life, but that it would last only for a few minutes or seconds.

On this man's forehead he left no imprint. Instead, he unbent the clutching fingers and left within them, for the police to find, the little cigarette lighter containing the seal of the Spider, New York's great uncaught killer. Would the police believe that they had, at last, caught their man—even if dead or dying? At least it would puzzle them.

And then Wentworth, almost at the last moment before the police reached the bridge, threw his legs over the rail and dropped, feet first, almost silently, into the water—to swim under the *Molly Ann* and join Ram Singh among the piles beneath the old pier.

CHAPTER 20
UNDER SENTENCE OF DEATH

WENTWORTH AND Ram Singh returned to the Park Avenue apartment in rather a bedraggled condition because of their swim from the *Molly Ann.*

Letting himself into the apartment quietly with his latch-key, Wentworth was surprised to find nobody in the hall. Master and servant passed quickly to Wentworth's bedroom without meeting a person, a piece of good fortune which Wentworth appreciated since it relieved him of explaining the wet condition of his clothing.

His master partly dressed in dry clothes, Ram Singh headed for his own quarters. Almost immediately he rushed back in a state of excitement.

"Van Sloan missie-sahib gone!" he exclaimed.

Wentworth dropped the collar in his hand. One look at his troubled and excited servant assured him that something very serious had happened. Partly dressed, he strode out of the bedroom and entered the music room where voices sounded. Here he found the inspector and a group of policemen in earnest consultation. A few words from the inspector told him all that was known.

Madame Pompé had brought a small time bomb in her overnight bag. She had excused herself from the dinner table for a few minutes and had set the bomb to explode. The explosion resulting in harmless noise and smoke, had caused all the men to rush to her bedroom. When they returned, Miss Van

Sloan and Madame Pompé had vanished. Investigation revealed that the regular elevator man had been knocked on the head and that the elevator had been run by a strange man who wore the regular man's uniform. Beyond that, nothing was known, and the best detectives on the force could discover nothing to indicate where Miss Van Sloan had disappeared to.

"And you policemen let this happen right under your noses?" Wentworth snapped. He turned away with an expression of utter contempt upon his stern face.

Nor did he wait for or expect any reply to his question. He returned to his bedroom and rapidly finished dressing, commenting angrily in Hindustani to Ram Singh upon what had happened. From a drawer he took a .45 automatic Colt and strapped it in a holster beneath his arm under his coat. The heavy weapon would send a bullet with crashing force and with a roar that the ears could feel. No longer did he intend to fight soundlessly with air pistols and with stealth. There was one man too many in the world, and that man must die.

Even in the height of his anger Wentworth had a revulsion of feeling. What of Nita? Could he aid her more if he did not fight? Not for a moment did he doubt that Dr. Quornelle had captured her, and the reason for that capture could only be to put him in Dr. Quornelle's power.

As if the thought had been conveyed to him telepathically Wentworth, at that moment, was called to the telephone and heard the voice of Dr. Quornelle speaking over the wire. The voice was not quite so suave as when Dr. Quornelle had been Mr. X, and few words were wasted.

"You wish to see Miss Van Sloan once more—alive?"

"Naturally." Wentworth controlled his voice, but his grip on the telephone made his knuckles turn white.

"Then you will meet Madame Pompé at the foreign newspaper stand in Times Square in half an hour… And come alone. If you are followed by the police, Miss Van Sloan will die!"

"I shall come alone."

The click of the distant receiver indicated that the connection was broken. What was before him Wentworth could only guess. Probably Dr. Quornelle intended to kill him. It might be a shot from an office window while he stood by the news stand on Times Square. It might be anything. But there was only one thing to do. He must go, and he must go alone. After all, he had more confidence in himself than in all the police systems of the world.

One more thing he did before he left the apartment. Underneath his vest he strapped the thin set of tools which were so cleverly designed for burglarious activity.

On his way out of the apartment Wentworth paused in the hall. Excited talk could be heard among the police in the music room. A report had evidently been received regarding the wholesale slaughter upon the *Molly Ann*. Wentworth turned to the door and was stopped by Ram Singh.

"Sahib?" the native boy pleaded, and Wentworth knew what he meant. "No, no Ram Singh." Wentworth answered, placing his hand for a moment upon the Hindu's shoulder. "You cannot come… I must fight this fight alone."

AND INTO the night Wentworth went alone, to fight one

of the cleverest and most dangerous criminals the world had ever known. And because of Nita he made quite certain that he did go alone and that he was not followed by any New York City detective. He traveled by subway, shuttling to Times Square and coming out of the ground into the bright electric glare of that famous square within a few feet of the foreign newspaper stand which had been mentioned as his rendezvous with Madame Pompé.

It was only about midnight, and hundreds of people still crowded the side walks on their way to midnight shows or to night clubs. Wentworth did not have long to wait. A taxi drew up at the curb and the door opened. Wentworth strolled over to it and entered, seating himself beside Madame Pompé and casually lighting a cigarette as he did so. The taxi moved off, heading south without any direction from Madame Pompé.

As they moved away a newsboy was shouting an extra.

"Poison gas ship on Hudson River! Spider kills gang before police arrive!"

Wentworth glanced at his companion. She was gorgeously gowned for the evening, as was her custom, and the back of the dress was cut very low. Once as she leaned forward and exposed her back to his gaze, Wentworth smiled. There was no trace of blemish upon her fair skin.

"Like my back better now?" she asked, noticing his smile.

"My compliments to Dr. Quornelle," Wentworth replied. "He is a wonderful artist with his make-up box."

"Yes," she said. "He worked on my back for an hour to make you think that he had whipped me."

Wentworth noted that the taxi was proceeding south on Broadway.

"Going any place in particular?" he asked.

"I can't tell you anything," she answered. "You must do what I tell you to do. Otherwise—"

Wentworth did not inquire regarding the "otherwise." Instead: "What will you take to sell him out?" he asked quietly.

Madame Pompé shook her head and was silent.

"Will you take half a million in cash?" he asked. "I think I could raise it tomorrow." He was thinking about Nita. It is doubtful if he ever would try to buy his own safety.

"No," she answered emphatically. "It is too late. I could not sell him out now, even if I wanted to."

Wentworth puzzled over the meaning which might lie behind her words and conversation ceased. The taxi was traveling farther and farther south on Broadway and they were coming to the great financial center of the world. Fewer people were upon the sidewalks in this part of New York. In Wall Street, itself, the heart of all money the world over, only night watchmen and caretakers are present during the night hours.

And it was into narrow Wall Street that the taxi finally turned from Broadway. It traveled a few short blocks and turned into a side street, stopping only a half block from the greatest financial street of the world.

Wentworth glanced through the window and saw that they had stopped before a large office building that had been boarded across the front in preparation for the wreckers. It was one of those buildings which had once been very important, but which was now about to be torn down to give place to a newer and more important structure.

"Remember," said Madame Pompé, as they left the taxi, "you are being watched every second. If you offer the least resistance, or make any kind of an attack, there is a certain young lady who will die."

It was all too true. On account of Nita, Wentworth was helpless. He followed Madame Pompé across the sidewalk to a door in the boarding, which opened easily at her touch. Inside the boarding they came to the front door of the building before which a man stood with a flashlight. This man turned without speaking, and they followed him into the building.

With his flashlight the man led them across the main hall and down some steps to the basement, Wentworth thought of the pistol in his holster. He expected to be searched and he expected to lose it if, indeed, he was not killed instantly without any search at all. But until he had found Nita, he could do nothing.

BEFORE SOME huge boilers, which had once heated the building, electric lights were burning and half a dozen men were playing cards around a rough table. As they came into that lighted basement room, Dr. Quornelle, himself, came out of some shadows and stood before Wentworth. The expressionless stare of the two men was pitiless, under the circumstances, in its very lack of expression.

"You understand, of course, Mr. Wentworth," said Dr. Quornelle coldly, "that I have arranged for your little Nita to die if you make the slightest resistance."

197

"Perfectly." Wentworth was smiling, acting superbly in the face of death and what, to him, was worse. "If I had not understood that, my dear doctor, you would have been dead five seconds ago."

Abruptly Dr. Quornelle patted his prisoner's clothing, discovered the automatic pistol and drew it from the holster. He did not, however, discover the thin kit of tools beneath Wentworth's vest.

"An excellent weapon," Dr. Quornelle commented, slipping the pistol into his own pocket. "I would kill you with it if I had not planned a more disagreeable end for you."

Wentworth laughed. "And what may that end be, Dr. Quornelle?"

"This way, my friend," replied Dr. Quornelle ironically. "I shall now take you to the young lady whom you seem to esteem so very highly as to give your life for her."

In the gloom across that portion of the basement, was an iron door, heavily bolted on the outside. The doctor opened the door. As he did so he covered Wentworth with a revolver.

"You will find the lady on the inside," he said. "Nita!" called Wentworth.

"Don't come in, Dick," the voice of Nita replied from the darkness of the room. "It's a trap!"

But Wentworth had no alternative. The odds against him were too great. For Nita's own sake he could not yet risk an encounter. He walked into the blackness of what seemed to be some kind of an old storage room and heard behind him the clang of the heavy door and the shooting of the big bolts.

"Nita!" he called, and she found him in the darkness and clung to him.

"Oh, Dick!" she sobbed while he held her in his arms. "Why did you do it? You must have known that they were only using me to get you. Why did you do it?"

He laughed and found her lips. "There is your answer," he said after a pause.

CHAPTER 21
THE SPIDER AMUCK!

THEY WERE interrupted by the voice of Dr. Quornelle which came through a grille in the iron door.

"Neither of you will ever come out of there alive," the doctor said malignantly. "As you die yourself, Mr. Richard Wentworth, you will have the exquisite torture of feeling the heart of the young lady stop beating under the influence of my poison gas. This is your punishment for interfering with Dr. Sylvester Quornelle, the man who will wreck the money kingdoms and hold the world in his grasp."

"It seems to me," drawled Wentworth in reply, "that you did not do much wrecking with the poison gas on the *Molly Ann*."

"Bah!" ejaculated the doctor venomously. "That was a small matter, a mere foreign-debt payment. "No ship could carry so much money as Wall Street holds. In the morning, when the banks are open, the deadly gas will flow out of my great boilers which are charged with it under high compression. Every human being within a mile of Wall Street will die, and the vast treasure

The heavy pistol continued to roar out its messages of death as man after man fell.

will be collected by my men who will wear the only masks ever invented to render this gas harmless."

"That gives us until ten o'clock in the morning," whispered Wentworth to Nita. "The banks do not open till then, and much can be done in so many hours."

Rapidly Wentworth began an examination of the small room in which he found himself. By sense of touch he discovered that it was constructed wholly of concrete and that it was windowless. It seemed as though the iron door gave the best chance for escape. Such a door, however, required more patience than skill. Without loss of time Wentworth selected a small drill from his kit of tools and began to drill a tiny hole at the height which, from memory, he judged one of the bolts to be placed. Once the bolt was definitely located, a larger hole could be cut and the bolt shifted from the inside.

Industriously he worked, oiling the drill frequently to render the drilling quite soundless. One of the bolts was located, and a hole was cut large enough to move the bolt from the inside when the right moment came. But the job was long and tedious and it became a race against time. It was a race for Nita's life and for his own life, as well as the lives of thousands of people in the great financial district.

Through the tiny grille Wentworth could see the group of men sitting round the card table. They had tired of cards and seemed to be dozing. Dr. Quornelle was not to be seen.

At nine o'clock in the morning, as indicated by the luminous dial of Wentworth's wrist watch, one bolt was ready to be moved.

But there was a lot of work to be done on the other bolt. The situation was desperate, if not quite hopeless.

Desperately Wentworth worked at his drilling while Nita crouched beside him and held the tube of oil which had almost been squeezed empty. Even if he did succeed in opening the door, Wentworth, unarmed, would have to face fearful odds on the outside.

Suddenly there was the distant sound of a shot. Another and another report sounded faintly. Dr. Quornelle came running within view of the grille.

"The police are attacking!" he exclaimed. "Two of our men are holding them off at the front door. Now, men, there is nothing to be afraid of. If anybody breaks in here, put on your masks and let the gas into the basement. But do not send it out through the manholes in the street before the banks open at ten o'clock. I am going up on the roof to turn the machine gun on the police. Remember your orders, and we can't lose!"

"But who told the police?" one of the men asked nervously.

"Bah!" barked Dr. Quornelle viciously. "Do as you are told and don't ask questions. The police probably traced us through the trucking company that carried our gas cylinders to the *Molly Ann*. But it's too late. They can't beat us now."

The little drill snapped as Wentworth pressed it against the iron. The others had already been worn blunt and useless. In the darkness of the little room, with Nita beside him and depending upon him, Wentworth realized his desperate situation. He dropped his tools and pressed Nita to him for a moment in silence. But it was only for a moment. His tools might be useless, but his mind was still working. And he never admitted defeat.

Outside Dr. Quornelle continued to reassure his men. "Remember," he said, "that we are impregnable. Nobody can beat us."

"I think I can." It was the cold, cutting voice of Richard Wentworth, speaking through the small grille in the iron door. "Do you remember the gas mask which you left by your safe in your boarded up house, Dr. Quornelle?"

Dr. Quornelle wheeled and strode swiftly toward the locked room from which Wentworth spoke. "What of it?" he snapped.

"I have it here," lied Wentworth and followed the lie with a laugh. "I had it hidden in my hat. I can live through your gas—and weeks, months or years afterwards I shall kill you, Dr. Quornelle!"

FURIOUSLY DR. QUORNELLE tugged at the big bolts, flung open the door and entered the room. In his right hand he carried Wentworth's .45 automatic. In his left he held a flashlight which sent a beam straight into Wentworth's face.

Wentworth sprang to one side, out of the beam of light, and crouched to spring. But the beam of light followed him instantly, and the pistol, behind it, held him helplessly within its menace. Again he sprang, and again the beam found him.

"Now where is the gas mask?" demanded the doctor.

"Come and get it," retorted Wentworth.

"I have no time to waste," countered Dr. Quornelle. "I'll shoot you now."

The heavy automatic rose into plain view beside the flashlight, both leveled at Wentworth. To spring seemed hopeless, yet there seemed nothing else for Wentworth to do.

"Drop that gun." It was Nita speaking, her voice low but determined. Into the doctor's back she was pressing the tiny heel of a shoe which she had slipped from her foot.

With a cry of rage Dr. Quornelle whirled and fired straight into the darkness behind him, not waiting to use his flashlight. At the same instant Wentworth leaped forward and seized the doctor's pistol arm just as the flashlight clattered to the floor and left the room in complete darkness once more.

It was then that Dr. Quornelle did a very clever thing. He dropped the pistol so that he might escape while Wentworth bent to grope for it in the dark. But both men were thinking fast. Wentworth had not heard Nita fall when the doctor had fired at her in the dark. He, therefore, depended upon her to obtain the pistol while he sprang after the doctor, just in time to block the closing door with his foot.

And Nita brought the pistol to him and the flashlight also almost immediately.

Outside Dr. Quornelle shouted to his men to shoot down the prisoners if they emerged from the little room. The next minute he had fled up the stairs on his way to the roof and the machine gun.

More shots sounded in the distance. Wentworth watched through the little grille, his foot still blocking the door. Still more shots sounded, and the men by the boilers began nervously to adjust their gas masks. One of them stood beside a valve wheel on a pipe leading into a boiler. It was this man who kept his gun pointed at the door behind which Wentworth stood.

"I am going out, Nita," whispered Wentworth. "Crouch down in a corner till it's over."

"Dick, you can't!" she whispered back. "There are too many of them."

"It won't be much of a gun fight," he reassured her. "They can't do good shooting while they wear those masks."

As he spoke, Wentworth flung the door.

THERE WAS a roar from his heavy pistol which drowned out a shot from the man by the valve wheel, who jerked backward and dropped dead. The heavy pistol continued to roar out its messages of death as Wentworth charged straight at the panic-stricken group by the table. Man after man staggered under the impact of the .45 caliber bullet which crashed through his chest or splintered its way into his brain. Seven men in all went down.

Nita, white with shock from the horror of the scene, staggered toward Wentworth. He caught her by the arm and half carried her up the stairs to the big entrance hall.

Much of the boarding had evidently been torn down by the police and considerable light was coming into the hall through the glass doors which had been badly shattered by bullets. Two men, crouching behind pillars, were firing through the glass of these doors.

Wentworth, unseen by the men behind the pillars, sprang onto the next flight of stairs with Nita. She crouched in an angle of the stairs while he slipped a new magazine of cartridges into the pistol and sent a bullet into each of the men below him. He could not tell how badly he had hit them, but he saw one of them jerk and the other one wriggle as he handed Nita his pistol for her protection and, weaponless, dashed upward to the roof in pursuit of his greatest enemy.

Wentworth followed the circling stairway which wound about the elevator shafts. Twenty flights of stairs are a stupendous feat to accomplish in a run. Yet he did it. Always in training, his muscles were superb, and the fury within him drove him as nothing else could.

Infuriated as he was, and with his muscles overtired, he paused abruptly at the top of the last flight of stairs to seize an opportunity which his ever-alert mind instantly recognized. At his feet was a disreputable coat, cast off by some workman, and beside it lay a battered straw hat. Quickly he discarded his own coat and donned the torn, black coat of the work man. He placed the ridiculous straw hat upon his head. One of his shoulders seemed to lower. Out upon the roof he hobbled, skipped and jumped—a horrible scarecrow of a man.

The Spider was attacking.

UPON THE roof there was already sounding the stuttering reports of a machine gun. Protected by a heavy iron shield from the windows of higher buildings, Dr. Sylvester Quornelle lay upon the edge of the roof firing downward with a machine gun which was cleverly braced by iron supports, so that it could be fired straight down into the street below.

Waving his arms and lurching grotesquely, the scarecrow of

a man approached the edge of the roof and looked down into the street where police lines were herding the masses of the curious out of danger from the machine gun. Still waving his arms the scarecrow tottered along the very edge of the roof so that people in nearby windows held their breaths. Apparently the man with the machine gun did not see the strange figure which was approaching him.

Slowly the wild figure came nearer to the maniac with the machine gun under the iron protection, then dived out of sight beneath that iron covering. The machine gun ceased its sputtering, and for a brief moment all seemed still upon the roof.

There followed a scream which could be heard by people in windows across the street. Into view, upon the roof, rose two men, the scarecrow and another man. Hundreds of people in neighboring windows stared horrified at the sight of those two, apparently maniacs, fighting to the death on the edge of the roof twenty stories above the street.

Richard Wentworth, in the ragged coat and broken hat, acted the part he was playing in the face of death as he fought Dr. Quornelle so close to the edge of the roof that it seemed certain they would both crash into the street far below. The two men struck and grappled, broke away and closed again. Twice they tottered, grappling, on the edge of the roof, and Wentworth had to save his enemy in order to save himself. Yet, if necessary, Wentworth knew that he would even sacrifice himself in order to defeat this man.

Then, suddenly, the two figures were down flat on the roof with the grotesque figure on top. Wentworth's steel-like fingers seized his enemy's throat and squeezed until Dr. Quornelle lay still. Quickly he took his cigarette lighter from his vest pocket, opened the secret compartment and bent low as he pressed the design of the vermilion spider upon the forehead below him. People in nearby windows thought that the man beneath him was being killed.

But the people were wrong. Abruptly the man in the ragged coat rose to his feet. He bent and lifted the other man, kicking and wriggling, straight above his head. For an instant the wild, misshapen figure held the wriggling man aloft, then tossed him, screaming, from the roof—to the police-cleared street below!

Rapidly Wentworth reentered the building, changed his coat and descended to Nita, reaching her as a flood of policemen surged into the entrance hall. They had only time for a word or two before Wentworth's friend, the inspector, found them seated side by side upon the first flight of stairs. But was the inspector still his friend?

"Mr. Wentworth," exclaimed the inspector, "a thousand people have just seen the Spider at work on the roof, and Dr. Quornelle is dead in the street with the spider mark on his forehead!"

"So?" Wentworth raised his eyebrows. "It seems to me, inspector, that the Spider is the best policeman in New York."

The inspector frowned. "Were you on the roof, Mr. Wentworth?" he asked, bluntly suspicious.

"My dear inspector," returned Wentworth, smiling, "if you wish to know what I have been doing, let me suggest that you go take a look at some dead people in the basement. However, they will wait while you search for the Spider!"

But in all the building the police found only one living person to place under arrest—Madame Pompé, hiding in a telephone booth.

There was no sign of the Spider.

POPULAR PUBLICATIONS
HERO PULPS

LOOK FOR MORE SOON!

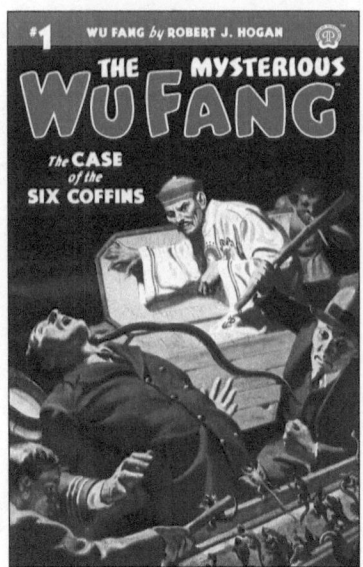

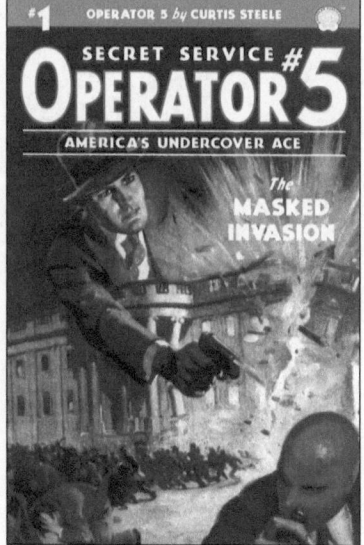